The Body In The Tower

By

Mark Reasoner

Standing outside Mr. Storm's drugstore on the west side of Craigsville's square, Corey Palmer checked the time like most folks did when the bell tolled from the courthouse clock.

Only three minutes off this time, he thought, *not too bad.*

Corey stood in the building's shade, trying to stay cool in the summer heat. He looked around the green common area as he waited for his friend, Michelle, watching people go into the businesses and offices on three sides of the square. The courthouse took up the entire north side.

"I wonder if the stupid thing was ever accurate," he said quietly to himself. He didn't hear Michelle approach.

"What was ever accurate?" she asked, startling her friend.

"The clock and the bell," Corey said, regaining a little composure. "The half-hour chime was three minutes late just now."

"I don't know," Michelle said, "my folks say the bell has always been off. And there's no rhyme or reason."

"It's weird," Corey said. "It's like we have our own time zone or we're out of sync with the rest of the world."

Corey opened the soda he'd purchased and stuffed the jelly beans he'd bought into the pocket of his baggy shorts.

"No Chocolate?" Michelle asked.

"Mixing it up," Corey replied. "Besides, they'll keep better in this heat."

They started walking.

Corey Palmer and Michelle Pritchard were neighbors, classmates, and best friends. Growing up within two blocks of each other, they'd attended the same elementary school and now middle school. Since teachers still assigned seats in alphabetical order, the two sat either next to each other or one behind the other since beginning first grade. As they'd been playmates even before going to school, their friendship seemed entirely natural.

Corey was taller than average for his age, slightly built with light brown hair and blue eyes. He might begin turning heads depending on how he filled out. For now, though, he was more child than man.

Michelle was small for her age, though not by much. Still mostly thin, she'd just begun the changes her mother warned about. Her hips were becoming slightly rounder and bra lines were visible under her usual tee-shirts. Her hair was more medium brown, darker than Corey's. She had green eyes and a few freckles across her nose.

Not that Corey noticed much of this. To him, Shel was just his best friend. She felt the same about him. They thought alike, played, studied, and worked together, and so far, no hormones lurked to complicate things. Not yet, anyway.

They were twelve years old and basically bored on this sunny June afternoon. School was out until August and neither was taking any summer classes. Seventh graders just didn't do that, or so they said.

"What do you want to do for the rest of the afternoon?" Corey asked.

"I don't know," Michelle said, "The library's closed for the rest of the weekend. There isn't anything going on at the park, and it's probably too close to dinner to grab our bikes and ride down to the lake."

"You want to go over to Bartram's?" Corey asked.

"Not really. They don't like it if you're just looking around."

"We could head home," Michelle continued.

"Nothing to do there," Corey said, "Nothing good to watch on TV and I'm already over my computer time for the week."

"Me too," his companion replied.

"Why don't we call Timmy or Paula? Maybe they want to do something," Corey said.

"I'd love to," Michelle said, "But we'd have to go home anyway. Mom took away my cell phone."

She told Corey how the latest phone bill showed way too many texts and almost a hundred extra minutes used. Her mother took the phone away for the rest of June.

"Is that why I had to call your land line?" Corey asked.

"Uh-huh," Michelle said. "So why don't you call them?"

Corey stopped and turned to his friend. He looked down at his shoes.

"My mom took my phone too. She caught me downloading too many games."

They walked on, reaching the corner. To their right was the courthouse, with city hall and the public safety building behind. Craigsville's police department and the Wagner County Sheriff's Office shared this facility, along with a common jail, run by the county.

"Let's wander around the courthouse," Corey said.

"Why?" Michelle asked.

"It's air-conditioned and there's a ton of stuff displayed," Corey said, "Old paintings, Civil War relics, plaques honoring old politicians and other people. And they've got a neat timeline on the history of this area."

"So what," Michelle said, "We can see that stuff anytime. And I've seen most of it."

"Yeah, but not all of it," Corey replied, "My mom told me they've changed a bunch of the stuff on display recently."

"Besides," he continued, "I want to see where they added my dad's name to the honor plaque. Come on, Shel, let's check it out."

"Okay, okay," Michelle said. They crossed the street to the courthouse.

Since it was still before five o'clock, no matter what the bell in the tower said, the building was still open to the public and the two youngsters strolled right in. They turned left from the entrance to begin checking out the pictures and other things displayed. On the long walls in this main area were plaques dedicated to the soldiers, sailors, and marines from Wagner County who gave their lives serving in the various wars throughout America's history.

Corey and Michelle looked at the ones listing servicemen from the Revolutionary War, the War of 1812, the Mexican War, and the Civil War, then they crossed to the other side to view the lists of those who died in the Spanish American War, World War I, World War II, Korea, and Vietnam. They finally came to the latest, honoring those who gave their lives in the Gulf Wars.

Corey didn't really remember his father. Staff Sergeant David Palmer died fighting in Iraq when Corey was only three. He'd seen pictures and his mother talked some about the man, but there weren't solid memories.

Corey stood silently in front of the bronze tablet. He traced his father's name and dates with his finger.

"I know it's sad," Michelle said.

"My mom really misses him," Corey said, "And I guess I do too, but I don't really remember much about him."

"Let's get out of here," Michelle said.

Corey turned to his friend. "No, it's okay. Besides, the newer stuff is upstairs. Come on."

They climbed up the wide staircase leading to the second floor. This was where the action happened. All the courtrooms were on this second level, along with the Judges' offices and chambers, along with conference and jury rooms. This was where the lawyers, witnesses, and everyone else hung out.

Corey's mother, Annette Palmer, worked up here for Judge Theodore J. Danielson. She was one of his clerks, so she sometimes actually worked inside the courtroom. Other times, she worked in the office, typing and filing, scheduling conferences and other things needed to keep the judge's work running smooth.

Though it was getting late for activity around the place, Corey knew his mother would be working until about six o'clock. He knew he should check in, but didn't want to take time right now.

He and Michelle began slowly walking down the hall, looking at display cases with antiques and relics from the city and county's history. There was a lot to see here.

They became separated as they walked and looked. Each was interested in different things, so one would move faster than the other for a while. Corey loved looking at the Civil War things like old surgery kits and Confederate Army hats. Michelle took more time with the things from the early twentieth century.

"So where's this timeline you were talking about?" Michelle asked as they came to end of displays.

"I'm not sure," Corey said, "I suppose it's on another floor. I guess we should ask someone."

"Ask someone what?" a man asked. The kids turned to see a tall, slightly overweight man approach them. He wore an open black robe and his gray hair was swept back as he walked.

"What are you looking for?" the man asked as he came near. He stopped about three feet from the two and looked seriously at them.

"You're Mrs. Palmer's boy, aren't you son?" He said.

"Yessir," Corey stammered. "I'm Corey Palmer and this is my friend, Michelle."

"Yes, indeed," the man replied, "Yes indeed. Glad to meet you. I'm Judge Barker. Now what are you looking for?"

"We heard there's a timeline of history on display here," Corey said, "But we don't know where."

"Well," the judge said, "It's actually up on the third floor, in a couple of big rooms. But you might want to hurry; they're probably going to close up pretty soon."

Corey and Michelle thanked Judge Barker and trotted quickly to the stairway leading up. When they got to the third floor, they quickly found the rooms. Unfortunately, the judge was right. The display was closed for the day.

"Now what?" Michelle said.

"I don't know," Corey said, "Let's see what else is up here."

The two walked back toward the center of the building. They tried each door, but all were locked. Then they came to a door in the center of the hallway, set back into an alcove. Corey tried the door.

It opened to reveal a stairway heading up.

"I wonder where this goes," he said as Michelle joined him.

"I don't know," Michelle said, "But I'll bet it's someplace we shouldn't go."

"Come on, Shel," Corey said, starting up the steps. "Let's find out. Besides, if they didn't want people up here, why is it unlocked?"

Michelle joined her friend. They climbed four flights to a small landing. On either side were closed doors. Both were locked.

"Storage closets, I bet," Corey said. On the wall opposite the stairs was a ladder mounted to the wall. Looking up, they saw a trap door in the ceiling.

"Hey, I bet that's the clock up there," Corey said. "Let's go up."

"No, Corey," Michelle said, "It's too dangerous."

"You're not afraid, are you?" Corey said smirking. Michelle didn't answer.

Corey climbed the ladder as far as he could. When he could reach the trap door, he held on to a rung and reached for the old metal latch. He tried moving it, but the rusted metal didn't budge. A few flakes broke off, drifting down.

Several steps lower, Michelle watched her friend's efforts. "See? We can't get up there anyway."

Corey kept trying to loosen the latch. "Hang on," he said, "I can get it." He kept trying to jiggle the black and rusty device. More rust flakes fell to the floor.

"I think it's moving," he said. And then it did. The latch came away from the door frame with a groan. Corey moved it to the inside of the whole mechanism and let go. It stayed in position.

Corey grabbed the ladder again and climbed another rung. With his head almost touching the wooden door, he pushed up as hard as he could. The door opened slowly. He climbed another rung and pushed the door open as far as he could. Grabbing the side of the frame, Corey climbed all the way into the upper chamber.

"Whoa," he said, looking around the dark chamber. He called down to his friend.

"You gotta see this, Shel," he said, "You won't believe it."

"What is it?" Michelle asked.

"It's the clock. Come on up."

Michelle climbed the ladder into the upper space; she stepped onto the old wooden floor and looked around. It was the clock alright. Four actually, as each side of the tower had a clock face. They saw the reverse side of the numbers through the large, translucent, white circles with each having a shaft extending from its center to a spindle and gear in the middle of the chamber.

All around this were brass gears of every size, cables, wires, and other pieces of machinery neither could identify.

Michelle tried to move toward the opposite side, but was blocked by the open trap door. She started to close it.

"Don't do that," Corey said.

"You set the latch open, didn't you? Michelle asked. "Besides, it's blocking us from moving around."

"Okay," Corey said.

Michelle carefully lowered the trap door into the floor. Unknown to both kids, Corey hadn't set the latch open. It was stuck open when they came up, but when the door hit the frame, the latch rattled just enough to engage its spring and it returned to its locked position.

Now they could see everything. There was little sound, though both heard clunks as large gears moved. There was also a low hum of an electric motor from somewhere in the room.

Corey began walking one way around the chamber and Michelle the other. They looked in wonder at everything. Sunlight came through the clock faces so they easily saw everything. Both of them easily walked under the shafts running from the center of each clock face. Obviously, the numbers and the hands were on the outside, Corey thought.

Above each face were louvered vents for air circulation. Screens covered the openings to keep birds and other critters out. Even with these, the air was hot and stuffy.

Meeting on the other side, they looked up to see a smaller platform with another ladder leading up to it. They could see some clockworks above.

"I wonder what's up there." Michelle said.

"I don't know," Corey said, "Why don't you climb up and see?"

"Why me?"

"It's your turn. I climbed up in here first."

"That's not fair," Michelle said.

"Aw, you're just chicken," Corey said.

"I am not!"

Corey clucked in reply.

Michelle raised her hand in a fist. "I'm going to hurt you, Corey Palmer."

Corey laughed. "Oh, come on, it's probably just more clockworks. I'll climb up after you. Nothing's gonna hurt you."

Michelle turned and climbed up. As she neared the platform, she could see the bottom of a large flat gear. It connected to a shaft leading down into the main works. She climbed past the gear edge to the platform and stood up. Brushing the dust from her hands, she turned and looked at the top side of the large gear.

Then she screamed louder than she'd ever screamed in her life.

II

No one beyond Corey heard, and he only heard the first half second of Michelle's shriek, because at that moment, the gear moved another notch and more gears and motors began working. Then the great bell hanging at the top of the tower rang out six loud and long peals marking the hour.

Michelle's screaming placed extra pressure on her eardrums from inside her skull, and this likely saved her hearing for the moment. The bell tolls were louder than a jet airplane at full takeoff power. Almost as loud as a typical rock concert, but inside the confined area, it echoed and reverberated extensively.

Standing on the lower floor, Corey heard his friend's scream followed by the bell's first bong. He reacted as most people would, by covering his ears with his hands as best he could.

As the sound of the last peal faded, Corey called out.

"Shel, are you okay?"

Michelle couldn't scream anymore, but she was still in shock.

"Corey! Omigod! *Corey*!" she rasped. Corey scrambled up the ladder.

Michelle sat on the platform with her hands around her knees. Her eyes were wide and she shook visibly.

"What's wrong?" Corey asked her, "What happened?"

Michelle couldn't speak. She just pointed shakily toward the large flat gear behind Corey. Corey turned and saw what freaked his friend out.

Lying prone on the brass was a very dead body. Not even much of one as little flesh remained on the bones. Whoever it was, whatever it was, it looked to have been there for a long time. Corey could see part of a face looking back at him through empty eye-sockets and saw what looked like leather covering what was left of the face. One bony arm was pointed straight out sideways and the other looked to be extended toward something, but the gears blocked Corey's view.

"Holy crap!" Corey said, "Is that what I think it is?"

"Mmm-hmm," Michelle muttered, nodding her head.

"Is it real?" Corey reached over to touch it.

"What are you doing!" Michelle screamed.

"I'm going to check it out."

"Are you nuts? *It's a dead body!*"

"It's not gonna hurt us and maybe we can find out who it is."

"It's gross and it's creepy," Michelle said, getting up from where she sat. "Let's get out of here."

She began climbing down the ladder to the main area. With a sigh, Corey followed.

Michelle got to the trap door first. Grabbing the metal handle, she yanked upward, but the door did not move. She tried again.

"What's wrong?" Corey asked.

"It won't open," Michelle answered, "I think it's stuck."

Corey moved to join her. He grabbed the handle and they both pulled. They felt a little movement, but the door still didn't open.

"Oh my god," Michelle said, "It's locked. I thought you set the latch open."

"I did," Corey said. "I'm pretty sure."

"Oh no!" Michelle cried. "We're stuck! We're trapped up here with no way out and we'll probably die." Her voice grew louder and more anxious and she stomped around the confined space."

"Take it easy, Shel," Corey said. "We'll figure something out."

"Like *what*?" Michelle said, coming back to where Corey stood. "We're locked in up here with no other door, no phones, no food, and there's some freaky dead thing hanging over our head!

"What are we going to do?"

Corey placed his hands on his friend's shoulders, but Michelle shook them off.

"We're gonna die," she whined.

"We're not gonna die," Corey said, "I'm sure someone will find us."

"Like they found that person?" Michelle asked, pointing up toward the platform they'd just climbed down from.

Corey didn't answer. Michelle went over to the wall of the clock chamber and sat. She wrapped her arms around her knees and lowered her chin to them. Corey sat beside her.

He felt something rustle in his pocket. He reached in and pulled out the bag of jelly beans he bought earlier at the drug store.

"Hey," he said, holding the bag for Michelle to see. "At least we've got something to eat."

She didn't reply. They sat silently for several minutes as the clock gears turned and clunked. The room wasn't completely dark as some light came in through the vents at the top of the tower and shown through the clock faces.

"Someone will find us, Shel," Corey said.

"They won't even look for hours," Michelle said. "My mom's working late, my dad's on the road, and I don't even have to be home until dark."

"Yeah, it's the same for me," Corey said. "I always liked that about summer break."

As the bell in the tower tolled what should have been six o'clock, Judge Danielson walked from his office to the larger part of his chambers where his staff worked. The judge, known as Theo to his friends and colleagues and Your Honor to most everyone else, usually wrapped the week up by four o'clock on Fridays. But today was different and he'd needed to hold some of his staff later than usual.

He let everyone go as they finished their work, and the only person still working was Annette Palmer. She was helping finish a backlog of filings, case briefs and other paperwork.

"That's the last of them," the judge said, setting another pile of folders on Annette's desk.

"Great, sir," Mrs. Palmer replied, "I can finish with them and get them down to the main records office."

"Forget it, Annette," Judge Danielson said, "They're closed for the day and Monday's fine. Go on home and enjoy your weekend."

"I'm just glad things should be back to normal next week," Annette said.

"You're right," Danielson said, "The calendar's light and Judge Rollins will be back."

He pointed to the pile of folders now on his assistant's desk and chuckled. "Not like this silliness. Over one hundred drunk & disorderly, public intoxication, and property damage cases all from one crazy high-school party."

"I'm just glad my son's not old enough to be part of something like that."

"But he will be someday, my dear," the judge said.

Annette looked up at the judge's smiling black face. Danielson was the only African-American Judge in Wagner and the surrounding counties. Since he was from a town in the same general part of the state, he easily fit into the county's close-knit community and no one made a deal about his race, milestone or not.

He was also the closest thing to an adult male influence in Corey's life.

Annette went to work for him after several years over at city hall, wanting more flexible hours. Unfortunately, flexibility cut two ways, as this week proved. Judge Danielson's court was booked solid dealing with all the cases arising from the out-of-control escapade some of the high school's seniors put together out by Lake Cyrus.

"By the way, Your Honor," she asked, "What have you heard from Judge Rollins? Is everything alright with her daughter and the baby?"

"Apparently so," Danielson replied, "They had to do a c-section, but everything worked out alright. Suzanne e-mailed some details, along with a picture of her new grandson."

"Now go on and get out of here," he continued, "These things will keep until Monday."

They said good night, and Annette left the building by a side door. On the way home, she stopped at the store to pick up some food and other things, arriving home around seven.

As she walked in, she called out for her son. "Corey, I'm home. Come here and help put up the groceries. Then we'll figure out something for dinner."

No answer.

She called again. "Corey, are you home?"

Silence again.

That's funny, she thought. *He knows I get home around now. Oh well, he's probably over at Michelle's. I can call later.*

She continued putting things away.

When Corey hadn't come home by seven-thirty, Annette began to be concerned. It wasn't like him, but still—with his absolute curfew being sunset, or at least to account for himself by then—it wasn't a crisis yet.

Annette decided to at least trace Corey as far as the Pritchard's. She dialed Michelle's mother.

"Hey, Annette," Mrs. Pritchard answered when her phone rang.

"Marybelle, is Corey over there at your house?"

"I couldn't tell you," Mrs. Pritchard replied, "I'm still at the library. It's inventory and I'll be here until at least eight. In fact, I thought Michelle would be with you all. Is anything wrong?"

"They're not here. And I'm kind of worried."

Marybelle Pritchard also became worried. "Have you called him?"

"Well, I would," Annette said, "but I took away his phone. You wouldn't believe how many apps and games he's downloaded."

"Oh yes I would, honey," Marybelle answered, "In fact I had to take Shelly's phone away too. She texts way too much."

The women were silent for a few seconds. Then Annette spoke.

"Oh my lord, that means we can't get hold of either one."

"Oh dear, you're right," Marybelle said. More silent seconds passed as the women gathered their thoughts.

"Tell you what. I'll finish up here and come over. We'll figure something out." Marybelle said finally. "In the meantime, check Corey's phone and see if anyone's been trying to reach him. Maybe their friends know where they are."

While Annette waited for her friend to arrive, she turned her son's phone on and checked for messages. There were a couple from earlier in the day. Still, though, maybe those kids would know where her son and Michelle were.

She called the numbers, but had to leave messages.

She looked through more of the phone's history, but nothing stood out.

Then she had an idea. The kids used text messages more than calls, so maybe there would be something in that history. She checked, but again didn't find anything current.

Good grief! She thought as she scrolled through just the past two weeks. *No wonder the phone bill was so high.*

A door opening caused her to look up. Marybelle Pritchard walked in and sat.

"Anything?" she asked Annette.

"No," Annette said, "but I have an idea. Maybe we could send a message to everyone they talk to or text and see if anyone's seen them."

"That's a great idea," Marybelle said. "You do that and I'll get us something to drink."

Annette opened the message window. She knew everyone who looked at her message would think it was from Corey. So she needed to write something kids would notice. Short and to the point, but without raising any alarms. She thought for several seconds, and then started keying:

> *From Corey's Mom—*
> *Have you seen Corey or Michelle P.? Have*
> *them call or come home.*
> *Text reply.*
> *Thx*

Annette hit the *send* button and put the phone down. Marybelle came back with two tall glasses of iced tea. The women drank the cool beverage.

"I guess now we wait," Annette said.

"I guess so," Marybelle answered, "but you know those two. They get doing something and lose track of time."

"Aren't you worried?" Annette asked.

"Kind of, but I'm not ready to panic yet. It's still light outside, and the kids know the rules." Marybelle sipped her tea.

"Besides," she continued, "they've probably both forgotten they don't have any way to check in. Let's see what happens with your message and wait until it gets dark."

"Then we can panic."

Annette smiled at her friend.

Corey's phone began buzzing with replies. Annette picked up the phone and started checking the messages. She ran through several as more came, but most said the same thing.

"Sorry, haven't seen them"

"Not at the mall"

"Haven't seen them today"

And so on. Only one gave any clue: *"Saw C & M on the square PM. Drg Str?"*

"What does this mean?" Annette asked, showing the phone to her friend.

"I'm not sure," Marybelle answered. She sounded out the last two letter groups.

"Drug stir? Oh—drug store. Someone saw them outside of Storm's downtown."

"Well, that's a start," Annette said. "We can call them to see."

"I'll call Betsy Clark," Marybelle said, "I think she was working today."

During the hour or so their mothers shopped and finished work for the day, Corey and Michelle sat silently up in the clock chamber. Corey kept checking his watch so he'd know when to cover his ears to block the bell's sound as best he could. At six forty-five, he began wondering what was going on.

"The bell's really messed up," he said.

"No it's not," Michelle said, "It doesn't ring at night. At least I've never heard it."

"Yeah, you're right." He stood up.

"This would be a great time to check out that body," he said. He moved to the ladder leading to the upper platform.

"Corey, don't," Michelle pleaded.

"Oh come on," Corey said. "I want to see if there's any clue. It's a mystery."

Corey began climbing. On the platform he looked over at the body on the large gear wheel. The face and head now faced the other way, up to where a large vertical gear's cogs meshed with the flat one's teeth. The body's legs faced the platform. Corey saw old high-topped sneakers covering what must have been what was left of the feet. Above the legs, Corey saw a lump on the person's left side. He tried to make out what it was, but couldn't. Walking to the edge of the platform, he measured the distance to the gear itself.

Not far, he decided, so he took a step back and jumped. He easily cleared the gap and now stood over the whole carcass. He could see one side of the face, or rather skull. Dried and desiccated skin covered the sunken cheekbone and the body's teeth protruded from what was left of the mouth.

Yuck! Corey thought. *That would scare anyone.* He looked away from the face and saw the extended arm caught at the wrist between the meshed gears at the other side.

I guess that's how he got trapped.

Taking a step toward the middle of the gear, he looked down at where he'd seen the lump. Left rear pocket. *A wallet, probably*, he thought. *Maybe it will tell who this was.*

As he reached down to check the pocket, the gears moved again, almost knocking him down. Corey kept his balance and carefully reached into the jeans pocket. He pulled out a brown leather bi-fold wallet. Having been surrounded by denim and away from the air, the leather was in fairly good shape. The hinge hadn't broken and the old cowhide was worn about the same as Corey's dad's old baseball glove.

Not wanting to lose his balance again, Corey quickly jumped back over to the unmoving platform.

"Hey, Shel," he called down, "I found something. Come take a look."

"No," Michelle said, "I'm not climbing up with that thing."

"Okay," Corey replied, making his way down the ladder. He went back to where Michelle still sat against the wall.

"I found a wallet in a pocket." He showed it to his friend.

"We shouldn't touch that. We'll get fingerprints on it."

"So what? We didn't kill the guy."

"It's still wrong. Besides, who knows what's on it."

Corey shook his head and opened the wallet. On the left side was a card slot with clear plastic window. Corey saw the word *IDENTIFICATION* in faded ink. Below a space were labeled lines for name, address, and date of birth. None of them were filled in. On the right side was another slot for cards. He reached his fingers into it and drew out a heavy paper card.

"Oh wow," he said, "Look at this."

"What is it?" Michelle asked."

"It's a library card. Really old, too. It's got a name and date and everything."

The small card had *Craigsville Public Library* printed across the top. Typed in the space below was a name, *Phillip E. Cooper,* and below that were the dates, *1961 – 1963.* The word *Adult* was printed in the lower left, and there was a signature in the lower right.

"Let me see." Michelle looked at the card. "Oh wow. My mom showed me cards like this. She said the library used to use these before they had computers."

"Yeah," Corey said, "and look at the date. Over fifty years ago."

"You mean that thing's been up there for fifty years?" Michelle said.

"Maybe," Corey said. Michelle took the card and looked more closely.

Corey opened the bill compartment. He found two one-dollar bills and pulled them out. Before he could look at them, Michelle punched his arm.

"Know what else?" she said. "He had to be at least twelve years old."

"How do you know that?" Corey asked.

"Because it says *Adult* on it. I just got my adult card this year, didn't you?"

Corey nodded and looked back at the bills he'd found. One looked like the normal dollars he spent each day, but the other didn't. Rather than green printing, the numbers and the U.S. Treasury seal were blue. He'd never seen one like that. Across the top of this were the words *Silver Certificate.*

"Look at this, Shel," he said, "I don't think this is real money."

Michelle looked at the dollar. "I just think it's old, Corey," she said. "Look at the date at the bottom."

The lower right showed the words, *Series 1957B.* Corey checked the other one. It had the words, *Series 1963A* in the same spot and the words *Federal Reserve Note* across the top.

"Wow, these are old."

"Anything else in the wallet?" Michelle asked.

Corey had the wallet in his left hand and the dollar bills in his right. Without thinking, he stuffed the bills into his pocket so he could check all the other slots. He found nothing.

"No, that's it."

He put the library card back where he found it and checked one more place. He slid his fingers behind the unfilled identification card and felt something. He pulled out a folded slip of paper.

"Hang on," he said. "Here's something else." He closed the wallet and put it in his lap.

"What is it?" Michelle asked.

Corey unfolded the paper. It was torn on one edge, and there was nothing on it except some faded numbers. He held the sheet up so light would bleed through and highlight the writing.

"It looks like some numbers," he said, "I think it says *5-9847.*"

"What's that mean?" Michelle asked.

"Beats me," Corey replied. "That's all it says. And there's nothing else in there."

"But at least we know his name," he continued, "Phillip Cooper."

"Yeah," Michelle said. They sat silently for awhile.

Feeling her stomach growl, Michelle asked Corey for some jelly beans. Reaching into his pocket, he stuffed the folded paper in with the bills as he took out the bag of candy. They split the beans evenly, though Corey took all the licorice. Michelle didn't mind, she liked the red ones best. They finished their dinner before the sun went down.

III

Most kids receiving Mrs. Palmer's text did not reply. Some didn't know anything, while others never got around to replying. A few didn't care, since they didn't really like Corey or Michelle.

Some kids had their phones turned off or silenced while eating dinner or doing other things. Jenny Wentworth thought she'd turned hers all the way off when she entered the theatre. It was only set to vibrate, and she felt it go off during the first half-hour of the blockbuster movie she was watching. Friday was movie night for the Wentworths and this week they'd included her grandfather, Judge Howard Barker.

Jenny reached for her phone, knocking into her mother in the next seat.

"No, Jen," her mother said, "It's rude."

"I know, Mom," the young girl answered, "I was just going to turn it off." She didn't read the text as she powered the device down.

The long summer day turned to dusk, then twilight, and finally dark. No more word came to Corey's phone, and while Betsy Clark did remember the kids buying some soda and snacks, it was much earlier in the afternoon. She didn't know where they went after.

"Okay," Mrs. Pritchard said, "I think we can officially panic. What should we do?"

"I'm calling the police," Annette said.

Craigsville had its own police department, but shared many functions with the Wagner County Sheriff's Office. One was night-time operations. While city officers patrolled inside Craigsville's limits and Wagner County deputies covered the outlying areas, dispatch and incoming calls were all handled by the county from the jail building.

Sergeant DuPree at the desk answered Mrs. Palmer's call.

"My son is missing," Annette told the officer, "along with another child."

"Yes, ma'am," DuPree replied. "Can you give me some details?"

Annette described the two children, trying her best to remember what Corey was wearing that day. Marybelle supplied details on how Michelle was dressed.

"When did you last see them?" the Sergeant asked.

"Not since this morning," Annette said, "when Mrs. Pritchard and I both left for work. But they were seen on the square this afternoon."

"They just never came home," she continued.

"Alright, Mrs. Palmer, I'll get the word out," DuPree assured her. "Please try to stay calm and remain by the phone."

"We'll do everything we can to find them."

Missing children weren't taken lightly in Craigsville. Though the community did pride itself on being relaxed and loose with rules on kids during the summer, letting them roam and play until sunset.

Daylight's end, however, meant everyone under the age of sixteen needed to be home or otherwise accounted for. Police officers throughout the city and county would stop any youngster out and about after dark, asking names, addresses and checking up on the answers. Most every child in the area could tell at least one story of being picked up and taken home in a police car.

So could their parents.

Even Sergeant DuPree knew the rules. Growing up in the area, he'd been stopped and questioned many nights when he'd stayed out a little too late. Sometimes he deserved it.

The sergeant acted quickly. He gave the information to dispatch and the call went out. The dispatcher radioed the basic information to every patrol and sent the details to each car's computer.

Sergeant DuPree then sent messages to others needing to know, including the Sheriff himself, the mayor and the county's chief judge.

Judge Barker and his family exited the movie theatre and began walking to their car. His granddaughter, Jenny, turned her phone on to see what she'd missed. The text from Corey's mom came up first.

"I wonder what this is about," Jenny said as they crossed the parking lot.

"What is it, sweetheart?" Judge Barker asked.

"A text message asking if I've seen some other kids today." She began reading other messages.

"Who are they looking for?" Her mother asked as the group piled into their car.

"Hmm?" Jenny said.

"Who are they looking for?" Mrs. Wentworth repeated, more sternly.

"Oh," Jenny replied, "Corey and Michelle."

"Now why do those names ring a bell?" Judge Barker said to no one in particular.

The Wentworths dropped the judge at his house and went home. Barker hadn't taken his own phone to the theatre, but checked it for messages and missed calls as soon as he closed the front door. No texts, but there were some voice mails.

He listened to Sergeant DuPree's first. As soon as he heard the names, the judge recognized them as not just the kids his granddaughter mentioned, but also as the two he'd run into in the Courthouse earlier.

Barker called the police station.

"I don't know if this helps," he told the sergeant, "but I recall seeing those two children at the courthouse earlier today."

"When was that, sir?" Dupree asked.

"Around five o'clock. I was headed for my chambers."

Sergeant Dupree added this to his notes. "That could help, Your Honor, it's later than the last time anyone saw them."

"Have you sent anyone over to see the parents?" Barker asked.

"No, sir," DuPree answered, "But that's really up to the chief or the sheriff. I'm sure they will."

"Alright, Sergeant, thank you. Please keep me informed." The judge hung up. He was fairly sure someone would get over to see Mrs. Palmer and Mrs. Pritchard, but with every officer probably looking for Corey and Michelle, it could be a while. Someone in authority needed to be with the mothers, and Barker knew just the right person.

He made another call.

At the Palmer's house, Annette and Marybelle waited. They tried to eat but couldn't. Annette kept drinking iced tea, but Marybelle switched to something stronger. It kept her more relaxed.

Around ten o'clock, Annette couldn't take not knowing anymore. "I'm going down to the police station," she said.

"No, honey, don't do that," Marybelle said. "Someone will call when they know something."

"Speaking of which," Annette said, "why haven't you called Pete? He needs to know."

"I know, but it wouldn't help anything," Marybelle replied. "He's over in Texas somewhere, probably taking his required break.

"All he could do is throw his logbook out the window and drive straight home."

"But even that wouldn't get him here much before mid-morning," Marybelle continued. "And what good would that do? I'd rather have him safe."

The doorbell rang and Annette went to answer it. She opened the door and saw her boss standing under the porch light.

"Judge Danielson, what are you doing here?" she asked, as she opened the screen door.

"Judge Barker called me about Corey and Michelle," Danielson answered. "He thought you might appreciate some support."

The judge joined the women in the living room. Annette offered Danielson something to drink, iced tea, or something stronger, but he declined.

"Have you heard anything?" Danielson asked when they were seated.

"Nothing," Annette said. "The last anyone saw them was this afternoon on the square."

"Well I've heard something," the judge said. "Judge Barker also told me he saw Corey and Michelle around five up in the courthouse."

"What were they doing there?" Marybelle asked.

"He didn't say," Danielson replied.

"Wait a minute," Annette said. "If they were at the Courthouse after five, why didn't we see them? We left just after six."

"They were probably gone by then." Danielson said, "After all, the place is locked up at six, and anyone still inside has to use the exit-only doors."

"But what if they didn't leave?" Marybelle asked. "What if they were still inside when the building was locked?"

"Corey's been there with me enough times," Annette said. "He knows how to get out."

"But has anyone checked?" Marybelle asked.

The three adults sat thinking for several seconds. Then Judge Danielson stood and took out his phone.

"There's one way to find out," he said. "I'll make some calls and we'll go down there."

This time the calls worked around in reverse order. Judge Danielson called Judge Barker to let him know and then called the building supervisor to unlock the doors. Judge Barker called Sergeant DuPree, the Sheriff, and city police chief. They agreed to send officers to help search.

Up in the clock tower, Corey and Michelle dozed. As darkness fell, their energy levels dropped too. Though the room wasn't totally dark, the only light came in through the vents at the top of the chamber. A few sounds came through as well, cars and trucks going down the streets, and an occasional siren sounded in the distance.

Michelle lay curled on her side with her head resting on her arm. Corey lay flat on his back with his head against the wall. They hadn't said much since finishing the bag of candy.

The search party gathered at the street level door on the back side of the building. Mrs. Palmer, Mrs. Pritchard, and Judge Danielson arrived first, just before Judge Barker. He needed to show where he saw the children, but also didn't want to miss anything.

Two officers joined the party as the building supervisor unlocked the door and everyone went in.

"I saw them up on the second floor," Judge Barker said once everyone was inside. "Though they might have gone anywhere after that."

"Why don't we split up?" Danielson said. "Mrs. Palmer, an officer and I will search the second floor, while Judge Barker, Mrs. Pritchard, and the other officer search the first floor."

"Mr. Hingstrom," he continued, referring to the building supervisor, "if you don't mind, why don't you search the basement?"

They split up, agreeing to meet again on the main stairs in thirty minutes.

Half an hour later, everyone gathered again. They'd searched every unlocked room, along with a few locked ones, such as the records office and others, but found no evidence of anyone being there who didn't belong. Judge Danielson and his companions checked his chambers, Barker's offices and all the courtrooms and conference rooms. They didn't find anything. All the other judges had left before five that afternoon, so they didn't unlock those areas.

"Okay, now what?" one of the police officers asked when everyone was together.

"The third floor," Judge Barker said. "I think that's where they said they were headed."

"What's up there?" the other officer asked.

"A new historical display, among other things," Barker replied.

"Mostly storage rooms and additional offices," Mr. Hingstrom added.

The group made their way to the third level. Splitting up, they quickly checked every room they could, with the building supervisor unlocking doors where needed.

Walking between two rooms, Mrs. Pritchard noticed the open door set back from the main hall. She called to the others.

"Where does that lead?" she asked.

"To the clock," Hingstrom answered, "and it shouldn't be open."

"We need to check," Judge Barker said.

Everyone climbed the four flights up. Gathering on the top level, Judge Danielson asked Hingstrom what the doors led to.

"These are the maintenance rooms," Hingstrom answered. "They hold the motors that run the clockworks, and it's where we oil the cables and set the timers and everything."

"What about up there?" Judge Barker asked, pointing to the ladder and trap door.

"That's the clock itself," Hingstrom answered. "But I don't think anyone's been up there in years."

"Why not?" Annette asked.

"No point," Hingstrom said. "We can maintain everything from down here and the clock hands and numbers are on the outside."

"Unless the whole thing blows up, nobody bothers."

In the tower, Corey stirred. He thought he heard sounds coming from below. Opening his eyes, he concentrated. Yes, there was something, or someone.

"Shel, wake up," he said, nudging his friend.

"Wha…?" Michelle said, turning over.

"I hear something."

"You're dreaming," Michelle replied, "We're stuck up here."

Another murmur came through the floor.

"There—did you hear it?"

Not waiting for a reply from his friend, Corey got up and went over to the trap door. He stomped his foot on the planking.

"Hey!" he hollered, *"Up here! We're in the Clock!"*

"Hey!"

The group below definitely heard Corey's yells. One officer quickly climbed the ladder and worked open the old latch. He pushed the trap door upward, almost knocking Corey over.

"Are you Corey Palmer?" the officer asked as he stuck his head into the chamber.

"Yes, sir," Corey said, "and we got stuck up here."

Corey and Michelle quickly climbed down the ladder. They hugged their mothers.

While relieved to see the children safe, both women were a bit angry too.

"What were you thinking?" Mrs. Palmer said. Her friend echoed the question.

"We were just curious, Mom," Corey said, "We just wanted to see what was up there."

"You know better than this, young lady," Mrs. Pritchard told her daughter, "You could have been trapped up there for ages."

"You two are lucky that people remembered seeing you around," Annette said, "You've got a lot of explaining to do."

"Why don't you get them home and fed first?" Judge Danielson suggested. "It's been a long evening."

Everyone agreed. As the building supervisor closed the trap door, Judge Barker spoke to him.

"Mr. Hingstrom, I want this trap door sealed up tight. We don't want this to ever happen again."

"No!" Corey said. Everyone looked at him.

"You can't do that! There's somebody else up there!"

"What are you talking about?" Mrs. Palmer asked.

"There's someone else up there," Corey repeated, "At least there's someone's *body*."

Mrs. Pritchard looked at her daughter.

"He's right, Mom," Michelle said, "We found a dead body up in the clock."

"Why don't you show us?" Judge Danielson said.

The judge, Corey, and one of the police officers climbed back into the clock chamber. Corey led them to the ladder leading to the bell gears and the officer climbed up to the small platform.

She looked over to the large flat gear.

"*Oh. My. God!*" she gasped.

IV

It took several hours for the police and fire-rescue personnel to carefully remove the body from the clock tower. Corey, Michelle, and their mothers left long before they finished. After giving their statements to the officers, the tired and dirty kids were released to head home.

Things were not pleasant on the trip. Both youngsters wanted little more than something to eat and time to sleep. Annette and Marybelle had different ideas.

"Would it be too much to ask just exactly what got into you and how you ended up trapped in that tower?" Marybelle asked as Annette drove down the dark and quiet streets. She tried to stay calm.

"Don't you know how dangerous things like old buildings can be?" Annette pressed.

"We didn't mean to get stuck," Michelle said.

"And no one got hurt," Corey added.

"That's not the point," Annette said. "You got trapped where no one could find you. You know better than that, Corey."

"But I didn't have a phone," Corey whined. "How could I get hold of anybody?"

"And I didn't have mine either," Michelle said.

Neither woman replied. They had a point.

At the Palmer home, Annette told Corey to fix sandwiches for everyone.

"Make yourself useful, young man," she told him. "I went shopping so there's plenty of food."

"But mom…" Corey said.

"But nothing," Annette replied firmly. "You need food and I need a few minutes to think some things over. Now scoot!"

Michelle went along to help. As the kids worked in the kitchen, their mothers tried to figure out what to do with them.

"I do not believe they put us through this," Marybelle said, "I think I lost ten years from my old age tonight."

"I know. I was scared half to death," Annette said. "But they do have a point, you know. Neither had a way to contact anyone."

"And it's going to stay that way," Marybelle said. "At least where Michelle is concerned. She's not getting her phone back until school starts."

"Hold on, Marybelle," Annette said, "How will she stay in touch with you?"

"I'm not going to let her out of my sight," Marybelle replied, "that's how."

"You might want to do the same with Corey," she continued. "That way he won't get Shelly in trouble again."

"Or vice-versa," Annette said. "Those two are always getting into things together."

"So what should we do?"

"Ground them until school starts."

Marybelle nodded agreement as Corey and Michelle came in with sandwiches and drinks for themselves and their mothers.

After taking time to eat the food, Annette explained her and Marybelle's decision.

"You two are grounded for the rest of the summer," she said.

"What?" Michelle exclaimed.

"That's not fair," Corey said.

"It most certainly is," Marybelle said. "You two scared the daylights out of us. And you got the police, the sheriff, and the judges involved, too. Do you think that's fair?"

"But Mom, come on," Corey whined. "What are we supposed to do? There's a whole summer left."

"That doesn't matter, young man," Annette replied, "You got stuck in the clock tower with no way to call for help. And you dragged your best friend along with you."

"And you're up to your neck too, young lady," Marybelle said.

"So here are the rules, Corey," Annette said. "Whether Michelle has to follow them too is up to her mother."

"No phone, definitely no games, and no computer unless it's school work and I check it out first. We can talk about TV when I get home each night. Also, you will go nowhere unless I approve, and there will be adult supervision."

"Those work for me," Marybelle said.

"But you took our phones away," Michelle said. "If we'd had them, one of us could have called and we wouldn't have been trapped for so long."

The women considered this. "Alright, you can have your phones. But only to call me or Mrs. Pritchard to check in."

"Can we at least talk to each other?" Corey asked.

Annette nodded. "Not that it will do you much good."

Marybelle also agreed to the phone rules. Then she told Michelle to finish up so they could leave. After they'd gone, Corey resumed his complaining.

"It's not fair, Mom," he said, "You and Mrs. Pritchard are taking vacation away from us."

"You should have thought of that before getting into this mess," Annette told him. "Actions have consequences, and your actions mean you're done running around unsupervised until school starts."

"But what am I supposed to do all day?" Corey asked. "Just hang around here and stare at the walls while you're at work?"

"You've got plenty of books to read this summer, Corey," Annette replied. "Use the time to get a jump on the school year."

"Yeah, right," Corey mumbled. "Then what will I do next week?"

"That's enough, young man. If you don't watch it, I'll haul you along to the courthouse each day and put you to work."

"Be more fun than hanging around here." Corey mumbled.

"Actually, that's not a bad idea," his mother replied, calling his bluff. "I'm sure Judge Danielson won't object and maybe you'll learn something. You can read your books, run errands, watch the trials, and if you behave, I'll see if you can use one of the courthouse computers."

"I will get you up at six-thirty on Monday," Annette continued, "Now get to bed. I'll let you sleep until eight this morning."

Michelle and her mother didn't speak while walking back to their house. But as Michelle got ready for bed, Marybelle explained what would happen later that morning.

"You might as well do something useful, young lady," Marybelle told her, "Your father won't be home until dinnertime, and there are a lot of books and things to organize and inventory. So set your alarm for six."

"Mom, what are you talking about?" Michelle asked.

"I'm talking about how you're going to spend the rest of today and maybe Sunday," her mother replied. "You're grounded but since I can't be here to keep an eye on you, you're going to the library with me.

"And you are going to work."

"That's not fair," Michelle whined.

"And frightening me and Mrs. Palmer by getting yourself trapped up in the clock tower with no way out *is* fair?"

Michelle didn't answer.

V

The area's only radio station, WMCJ in Morris, didn't broadcast live after six in the evening, using a feed from its parent station upstate to fill the overnight hours. The station did have an engineer on duty to keep an eye on things and to take calls in case something important happened in the four counties the station served. Mostly, this meant scores and highlights from Friday night football games, along with occasional crazy happenings like major accidents, lost dogs, or lost children. The night guys would take notes and leave them for the morning hosts to broadcast. It made things seem less canned.

Bill Clancy heard Sergeant DuPree's broadcast about the missing children on his scanner and made a note. When midnight came with no update, he called the sergeant for an update. Dupree told him the kids were safe and gave a few details about where they were found and the body. Clancy wrote it all down for the morning crew.

Changeover to live broadcast came at seven Saturday morning. Station identification, a five minute news summary, and then Charlie Clyde started his show with the weather and other local notes.

"Good morning, everyone, and happy Saturday. This is Charlie Clyde with you on WMCJ, Hit Country 106-FM, bringing you the best in country music, along with news, weather, and whatever else comes along. It's a gorgeous summer day here in the four counties, with clear skies in the forecast and temperatures about where you'd expect them.

"Highs today should be around eighty-nine here in Morris and about the same over in Tyrone. Creek City might hit ninety and so will Craigsville.

"Speaking of which, it looks like some interesting doings over there last night. The Wagner County Sheriff's Office reported a couple of kids missing, but they turned up safe and sound by

midnight. Apparently they got themselves trapped in that old clock tower at the courthouse.

"Appears they also found something else. Folks are reporting a body was discovered up there as well. We don't have many more details, but we'll keep try to keep you posted. Meantime, let's kick things off with Miranda Lambert's latest."

With that, people began learning about Corey and Michelle's experience. Folks talked, texted, and gossiped through the morning, and word spread fast. By Saturday afternoon, most everyone in Craigsville, Wagner County, and the other counties in the area knew about the grisly discovery. Some e-mailed or texted the kids for details and other people called to hear the story first-hand.

Neither Corey nor Michelle knew any of this because by that time, they were well and truly into being grounded for the rest of the summer. All the messages went unanswered.

Corey spent the day shadowing his mom helping with chores, cleaning his room and working in the yard. By dinnertime, he was tired, dirty, and ready to sleep for a long time.

Michelle had it worse. She spent Saturday loading and unloading boxes of books and things for the library staff to organize and catalogue. She tried to help by putting each stack she unloaded into alphabetical order, but stopped when told she could only do that with the fiction books. Everything else needed to go by the Dewey Decimal sticker on the spine. At least there was pizza for lunch.

That evening, she had to tell her father everything.

"Why didn't you call me?" Pete Pritchard asked his wife when he learned what happened.

"And what good would that have done?" Marybelle asked. "You were still eight hours away, and I didn't want you taking chances getting home.

"If things hadn't worked out, I would have called."

Once he got past his initial anger at not being told Michelle was missing, Pete spoke more calmly to his daughter.

"Well, kiddo," he said, "you messed up. Granted, no one was hurt, and maybe you'll have a story to tell later."

"But you have to be more careful," he continued more seriously. "It's like my old trainer said, don't go faster than your guardian angel can fly."

"I know, Daddy," Michelle said, "and I'm sorry. But I still don't think it's fair that I'm grounded for the whole summer. Can't you do something?"

"Michelle," Mr. Pritchard said, "as long as I'm working this job and gone so much, your mother's in charge. I'm not saying I agree or disagree with her, but it's her call and I'm going to back her up."

"Learn the lesson, sweetheart," he continued.

"And Corey's grounded the same way," Marybelle said from the doorway to the kitchen.

"But I'm stuck here, aren't I?" Michelle asked.

"Not necessarily," Marybelle said, "we're just about done at the library, and so if you don't want to come with me tomorrow, you can go to church with the Palmers."

"Or you can help me in the garage," Mr. Pritchard said. "There's a lot to do out there and I can use your help Monday too."

Michelle went with Corey and his mother on Sunday morning.

After the service, the two stood outside and commiserated.

"I spent all day yesterday doing chores," Corey complained.

"Well, at least you were home," Michelle said, "I had to go with my mom to the library and she put me to work all day. And tomorrow I have to stay home with my dad and help him do the yard work."

"It's better than what I have to do," Corey said. "I have to go with my mom to the courthouse and hang around there all day."

"What will you do?" Michelle asked.

"I dunno," Corey said. "I guess I can read the books we're supposed to finish before school starts. But I'm almost done with the list."

"Me too," Michelle said.

"This sucks," Corey said.

"Yeah, but what can we do?" Michelle said, "They won't let us do anything without approval or supervision, and we can't even use our phones or computers. All I can do is hang out at the library and read or help around our house."

"I know," Corey said, "but at least we can keep in touch with each other."

"Hey," Michelle said, getting an idea, "since we're both grounded the same, and can't do anything else, maybe the folks will let us be grounded together."

"What do you mean?"

"Simple. Let's ask if we can hang out together either at the library or the courthouse or whichever house where one of our moms are home."

Corey agreed they could at least ask, so they brought it up on the drive home.

Mrs. Palmer didn't object, but made it very clear to Michelle she would have to follow the same rules Corey did while at the courthouse. They asked Michelle's parents later and the Pritchards also agreed. The kids would start their joint grounding on Tuesday at the library.

While Michelle helped her father with yard work on Monday, Corey spent his day in Judge Danielson's office with his mother and the rest of the Judge's staff. He ran his first errand when he helped Annette take all the case files from Friday down to the main records office. It only took one trip, and the head clerk made a small fuss over the young man.

They were still downstairs when Judge Danielson arrived and then quickly left for the weekly judicial meeting in the conference room. When he returned, he told his team they had a light week.

"We've got two hearings on Wednesday, but both should be quick, and the Lyman case is set for pre-trial motions on Thursday. I'm hoping they'll push the trial back until after the break. Otherwise, we may have to get it re-assigned."

"That's it everyone, let's carry on," he concluded. Then he noticed Corey sitting against the wall.

"Just visiting, young man?" he asked.

"No, sir," Corey said, "Not really."

Mrs. Palmer explained why her son was in the offices. As she'd guessed, the judge was okay with Corey being around. He even approved Corey using a computer as long as he didn't get in anyone's way and cleared any Internet sites with his mother.

As the County Courts and other offices started the work week, the medical examiner, Doctor Maureen Driscoll, began her autopsy of the desiccated and mummified body. She'd come in on Saturday to take custody of the remains and the few effects. The corpse spent the weekend peacefully in a drawer, but that was about to change.

First, Dr. Driscoll carefully removed the clothing and shoes, placing each item into a separate bag. As she did, she checked for anything in pockets, but only found the wallet Corey looked through earlier.

"So, Phillip Cooper," she said, finding the old library card. "I suppose this will do for now as ID."

Dr. Driscoll then began carefully opening the chest cavity, slicing through what was left on the bones. She noted the mangled right wrist, comparing it to the photographs taken at the scene. More examination revealed a skull fracture on the right side.

Since the human body is mostly water, there wasn't much left to work with. Just about all the muscle tissue and internal organs were shriveled away into unrecognizable lumps. Still, she knew where things should be and labeled each small lump accordingly. The only part of the body undisturbed was the teeth. She took photographs and made extensive notes as she worked.

Wagner County didn't have a full scale pathology or crime lab. Dr. Driscoll did what she could, but she would send most of the samples, scrapings and other things to the state crime lab. They would do what they could, but she wasn't hopeful.

At least maybe the dental work will identify the person, she thought. She looked more closely at the teeth.

"Interesting," she said out loud to herself. "No fillings. Either you took really good care of your teeth, or these were so new you never had time to get a cavity."

After finishing the work, she boxed all the samples and such, included a copy of her report and notes, and addressed the package to her main contact at the state lab. She kept her original report and notes, but made additional copies for the sheriff's office and the city police. Then she put the remains back into storage. Unless someone claimed them, or a definite identification was established, they'd stay here for several months.

On her way to lunch, Dr. Driscoll dropped both files off at the public safety building. Sheriff Wingate was finishing a sandwich when she walked in.

"What do you have, Mo?" he asked as she set the file on his desk.

"My initial report on the clock tower body."

"Anything interesting?"

"Not so much," Driscoll replied, "No evidence of foul play. Everything's consistent with an accident."

"Any idea who it was?" The Sheriff asked.

"Sorry, Abe, the only thing I found was an old library card. Nothing to clearly ID him."

"What else did you find?"

"Nothing else really." Driscoll said, "I'm not equipped to do detailed tissue analysis, DNA or things like that. I sent everything up to the folks at the Capitol and we'll know more when their report comes back."

"When will that be?"

"A week or so, it depends on how busy they are." Driscoll said, turning to leave.

"Could you run a copy over to the city police? They were involved, too."

"Already did, I ran into the chief on my way here."

"What did he say?"

"Nothing. He just said he'd read it." Driscoll began walking out.

"I really have to go, Sheriff, I've got a lunch date and I'm late."

"Thanks, Doc," Wingate said as the doctor left his office. "And by the way, did you send a copy to the judge?"

"Which judge?" Driscoll said, turning back to the Sheriff.

"Either Barker or Danielson," Wingate replied, "Can't remember which. They were both there when the body was found."

"Okay," Dr. Driscoll said, "I'll send a copy to each one. Gotta go."

Leaving the building, the doctor made a note to herself. She would send copies to both judges, but would wait until she could send a complete and final one.

After the medical examiner left his office, Sheriff Wingate opened the file and turned to the summary page.

Summary

Subject is a juvenile Caucasian male approximately 12-15 years of age, found prone and face-down on a large flat metal gear in the Wagner County Courthouse clock tower.

Height measured at 5'1" and weight estimated at 95 -100 lbs. Weight determined by measurement of bones and remaining skin, examination of subject's clothing for sizes and comparison to applicable anatomical tables.

Subject appears to have expired approximately 50 years ago, based on decomposition rate of the remains and mummification of tissue. Subject's clothing and personal effects are consistent with said time frame.

Subject's remains show no evidence of any disease, degenerative condition or other medical issues.

Two major injuries were noted during examination. First: a massive trauma to the right side of the skull, likely caused by extremely hard contact with a large flat and blunt surface. Second: subject's right wrist was severely mangled, consistent with being trapped and severely compressed between two heavy objects.

No identification found in personal effects, save for a Craigsville Public Library card listing the name, Phillip E. Cooper, and dated 1961 – 1963.

Fiber samples from clothing, photographs of shoes and belt, along with bone and tissue samples from internal organ remains sent to State Forensic Laboratory for more detailed analysis.

Conclusion

Cause of death is likely an accidental fall onto the large flat gear works in the upper portion of the clock tower. Injuries show no evidence of foul play and are consistent with a fall.

Neither injury should have caused the subject's death, though the head trauma could have resulted in unconsciousness. Coupled with the shock and possible internal bleeding caused by this injury, death may have resulted after the passage of time with no medical attention. Additional blood loss may have been caused by the injury *to the wrist.*

Further details to be added after results of state lab tests are provided.

His phone rang as he finished reading. He picked it up and said hello.

"Morning, Abe, Bob Blaise. Had a chance to read Doc Driscoll's report?"

"Just finished it, and you don't waste any time, do you Chief?"

"You taught me better than that, Sheriff."

Wingate chuckled.

"So what do you think?" the chief asked.

"Not much," Wingate replied "There's no evidence of foul play, and no clear identification. What's there to do?"

"I suspect there's an open missing person's case file somewhere," Blaise said.

"Maybe, but where would it be? And more important, *when* would it be?" the sheriff said. "Driscoll's report said the young man expired over fifty years ago."

There was silence for a few seconds.

"I guess you're right, Abe," Chief Blaise said, "I doubt if we could find anything after all this time. Still, though, something might turn up."

"It might, but I doubt it." Sheriff Wingate said. "Anyway, the doctor is sending her report to the two judges as well. I guess we can let them decide if there's something to follow up on."

After hanging up with the chief, Wingate closed the file and set it aside.

"*Well, young Mr. Cooper,*" he said to himself. "*If that's who you are, I'm truly sorry you had to wait so long to be found.*"

"*I also wish I could do something about it, too. But it looks like your death will remain cold for now.*"

Wingate picked up another file on his desk and began reading.

VI

Corey and Michelle spent the next day at the library, working through part of their required summer reading list. They didn't talk much since library rules said to be quiet.

On Wednesday, they were at the courthouse. They sat in the back of the courtroom during the morning while Judge Danielson dealt with three different matters. Two were scheduled, but the third needed the judge to rule on something about a man being evicted from his house and land. Neither youngster could really follow the arguments.

Back in the judge's offices, Corey asked his mother a question about something he'd heard.

"Mom, what does excla... excah-pah..."

"Exculpatory," Michelle said.

"Yeah," Corey said, "exculpatory. What does that mean?"

"Why don't you look it up?" Judge Danielson said, walking past. "There are books and references all over the office you can use."

"Oh," Corey said, "okay."

"It's how we do things, young man," Danielson said. "And besides, you might learn something new."

Using the law books and other references, along with the computer, Corey and Michelle did find out what *exculpatory* meant. They also learned some other complicated legal terms and wrote them down. At least they learned how to pronounce most of the terms, along with some sort of definitions.

"I'm going to drop these on my history and social studies teacher next year," Corey said, smiling.

"Not all of them," Michelle said. "Leave some for me."

It was back to the library the next day and the courthouse again on Friday. By then, though, the kids began to think being grounded together wasn't such a great thing. The whole thing began to wear thin, and they started getting on each other's nerves.

At least the next week would be a short one. Independence Day fell on Thursday and many city and county employees took Friday off too. It made the long weekend a nice mid-summer break. The judges tried not to schedule full trials during the short week and tried to keep other proceedings to an absolute minimum. Several judges, including Judge Danielson, took the entire week off. Their staffs did too, if they had the vacation days, but otherwise used the days to catch up or take things easy.

By Wednesday, Annette noticed the two kids were driving each other nuts. They weren't even speaking to each other on the ride home that day.

A long weekend and a break from each other might be good, she thought. Then she remembered tomorrow's get-together.

For almost forty years, Craigsville held an afternoon parade to celebrate the Fourth of July. It began at the old high school and wound down Centre Street to the square. After it ended, everyone went home, but came back in the evening to watch fireworks.

By the eighties, though, interest faded as expenses rose and the city couldn't afford the parade any longer. The high school was gone by then, consolidated into the newer Wagner County High with several other schools in the area.

But the city didn't stop celebrating. The annual fireworks show continued, preceded by a picnic and lawn party on the square. Things kicked off around six in the evening as people started showing up with lawn chairs and baskets of food. Some brought just enough for themselves while others brought extras to share. Folks ate, chatted, listened to music, played games, and had a relaxed good time until the fireworks started around nine-thirty.

Most years, they went off from the parking lot behind the jail, arcing over the courthouse tower and exploding way above the crowd. In drought years, or times with extreme wildfire danger, the city just moved the whole thing up to Lake Cyrus and shot the fireworks from a platform in the middle.

This year's party was downtown, with a local country band providing a short concert while people ate and socialized.

Like most years, Annette and Marybelle pooled resources and fixed a spread for both families. Pete Pritchard was home too, and though he had to leave on his next run early Friday morning, he wasn't going to miss the fun. Corey and Michelle ended up spending more time in close contact.

They hardly acknowledged each other as they ate sandwiches, potato salad, and chips. Their mothers did let them escape a little, allowing the kids to wander off and talk to other groups. But only if they stayed within view.

As darkness came and things began wrapping up, Corey and Michelle sat sulking in their lawn chairs. Neither spoke to each other or to the adults.

"What is wrong with you two?" Pete Pritchard finally asked. "You've been a couple of grumps all evening."

"Nothing," Corey muttered. "I'm just sick of this."

"Me, too," Michelle said. "And it's not fair."

"Excuse me, young lady," Marybelle said. "We've had this discussion. It most certainly is fair after the fright you two gave us.

Getting trapped in the clock tower where no one could find you. Good lord—do you think we're going to let you out of sight to get in that kind of trouble again?"

"But Mom," Michelle whined, "it wasn't my fault! It was Corey's."

"*What?!*" Corey said. "Uh-uh! You're the one who locked us in."

"But you should've set the latch open," Michelle said. "And it was all your idea. *You* were the one who wanted to go over the courthouse."

"I never wanted to look at the stupid history stuff anyway," she continued, "And then *you* got us into the stairwell, and *you* climbed up into the clock and messed with the latch. And *you* were the one who said to climb up to where that creepy dead body was."

"It's *all your fault*! And now I'm grounded all summer, too," Michelle said, facing Corey directly. "I *HATE* you, Corey Palmer!"

She sat down and folded her arms across her chest.

No one spoke for several seconds, but Annette saw Corey turn red and begin forming a fist.

"That's enough," she said to her son. "We will talk about this later."

"Indeed we will," Marybelle echoed.

Pete Pritchard leaned over to his wife. "Well, some of y'all are gonna talk later. I get to take off in a few hours."

Marybelle punched her husband's arm. "Now *that's* what's not fair."

"Now, darlin', don't worry. After I get back, I've got five days off. I'll keep an eye on things." They smiled at each other.

Neither Corey nor Michelle saw much of the fireworks display. They both sat silent in their chairs, staring at the grass, as the rockets exploded and sparkled overhead.

When Judge Danielson entered his offices on Monday, everyone was busy getting organized for the week, talking about their holiday happenings or just picking up where they left things the previous Wednesday. Corey slumped on the couch.

"Good morning, everyone," Danielson said, "Hope y'all had a good week and holiday."

"Yes, sir," "It was fun," "Enjoyed it," "Good to take a break," everyone replied.

Danielson turned to Annette. "Anything I need to know before the conference?"

"No, sir," she said, handing him a stack of correspondence and such. "Nothing urgent, just these things from late last week."

"Great," he replied. He turned and saw Corey.

"Good morning, Corey. Still with us, I see."

"Yeah," Corey grunted.

"Where's your girlfriend?" the judge asked.

"She's *NOT* my girlfriend!" Corey snapped. "She's not even my friend."

Danielson turned to Annette. "What happened? A bad break-up over the weekend?"

"It's a long story," Annette said.

Danielson went into his office. He laid the stack of things on his desk. He'd deal with them later, after the weekly conference. He didn't notice the label on a large manila envelope near the bottom. It was from the Wagner County Medical Examiner's office.

After the weekly meeting, Judge Danielson began working through the pile of letters and other things. He glanced through the medical examiner's file, but put it aside to read later at home. As he read other items, loud voices came from outside his chambers.

"Hey kid, you can't just take over someone's desk. Get out of here!"

"But I'm just trying to— " Danielson recognized Corey's voice.

"I don't care! You're in my way, and you're starting to get in everyone's way. Now move it!"

"Corey!" the judge heard Annette call. "Get over here and sit down."

"But Mom—" Corey said.

"But nothing!" Annette replied. "You sit down and behave or I will take you home and lock you in."

Danielson got up and opened his door.

"Okay, everyone, settle down," he said, stepping into the outer office. "What's the problem?"

"Nothing, sir," Annette said. "It's taken care of."

Danielson saw another staff member trying to stay hidden behind his cubicle wall. He knew this was who Corey was arguing with. He turned to Corey who sulked on the sofa.

"Um-hmm, I see," he said. "If it's all taken care of, then let's get back at it."

He walked to the sofa. "Corey, why don't you grab a soda from the fridge and then you and I will take a walk."

The judge's look told Corey it wasn't really a request.

A few minutes later, they sat on one of the benches in the hall, far down from Danielson's offices.

"Alright, Corey," the judge said, "would you like to tell me what happened back there?"

"I just wanted to look at something," Corey said. "You said I could use a computer."

"I also said you weren't allowed to get in anyone's way," Danielson replied. "And we do have work to do. So you need to be more aware and more considerate as long as you're here. Do you understand?"

"Yessir," Corey said, hanging head.

"Good," the judge said. "I also think you owe Rob an apology."

Danielson turned to look at Corey.

"Now then, what I really wanted to ask you is where your usual running partner is. Did something happen?"

Corey kept looking down.

"What happened, son?' Danielson said. "Did you two have a fight or something?"

"Yeah," Corey said quietly.

"You want to tell me about it?"

"She said it was all my fault," Corey said, looking up at Danielson. "She said she hated me." Corey told the judge about Michelle's blow-up at the picnic.

Danielson laughed. "She probably doesn't hate you, Corey. But I'd say she's pretty mad at you."

"But it's not true," Corey said, "it was just an accident.

"And besides, she was the one who closed the trap door getting us stuck up there."

Judge Danielson put his hand on Corey's shoulder.

"Now that may be true," he said, "but I think there's a little more to it."

"What do you mean?' Corey asked.

"Well, from what I remember about that night, it really was your idea to climb those stairs and then up into the tower. And I think it was also your idea to go up to the bell works above. Am I right so far?"

"Yeah, but..."

"And didn't you say you thought you'd set the latch so it wouldn't lock?"

"Uh-huh"

"But it just didn't work, did it?"

"No."

"Well then, Corey," the judge continued, "it looks to me like Michelle is sort of right. If anyone's at fault, it's probably you, don't you think?"

"Yeah," Corey said, "I guess so."

He looked up at the judge. "So what do I do?"

"Well," Danielson said, "The first thing you do is apologize. Then we see what she says."

"Do I have to?" Corey asked.

"Don't you want to stay friends with her?"

Corey nodded.

"Then you have to."

"And let me give you another reason," Danielson continued, "I've got something I wanted to show the two of you about the body you found. But I don't think it's fair to only show it to you. So let's get your partner back and we can see what we've got. Okay?"

"Okay." They went back to the office. Corey apologized to the staff member and the afternoon passed quietly. That night he asked Annette's permission to use his phone.

"Why?" she asked.

"I need to call Michelle."

Annette gave Corey a raised eyebrow look, but let him call. He dialed and waited for Michelle to answer.

"Hello," she said.

"Hi, Michelle," Corey said, "It's Corey."

"What do you want?"

Corey took a deep breath before speaking. "I wanted to apologize."

"Really?"

"Yeah, really. You were right, Shel, it mostly was my fault. And I'm sorry."

Michelle was silent.

"And I don't want you to be mad at me," Corey went on, "I want us to still be friends."

Michelle still didn't say anything.

"You don't really hate me, do you?" Corey asked.

"No, I don't hate you," Michelle said, "and I'm sorry too."

"What for?" Corey asked.

"I shouldn't have gotten mad. It wasn't anybody's fault. We just got stuck."

"Yeah," Corey said. "So we can still be friends and still hang together?"

"I guess," Michelle said, "if you want to."

"Cool," Corey said. "And if you come to the courthouse tomorrow, Judge Danielson said he had something to show us about the dead guy. Will you come?"

"What's he want to show us?" Michelle asked.

"I don't know," Corey said. "But he told me he'd only show it to both of us. So will you?"

"Sure."

They hung up. Annette saw Corey smile for the first time in a couple of weeks.

VII

The next morning, the judge's office was a whirlwind. The Lyman trial started that day, so most of the staff would be with the judge in the courtroom. Everyone else scrambled to keep all the other work going.

When Mrs. Palmer, Corey and Michelle arrived, Annette quickly grabbed what she needed and left for court. The kids brought books to read, but first asked when they could talk to the judge.

"I don't know," Annette said. "I will ask him when I get the chance." Then she saw the note addressed to Corey and Michelle on her desk. She gave it to her son and left.

Corey opened the note.

"Stick around at lunch, you two," it said, *"We'll talk then."*

They knew it was lunch when everyone streamed back into the office. Judge Danielson walked quickly into his chambers, motioning for the kids to follow. Once there, he sat down at his desk and picked up a file.

"This is what I wanted to show you," he said. "It's the complete report on the body you found in the tower." He placed the folder where Corey and Michelle could get it.

"Are you letting us have it?" Corey asked.

"No," the judge said, "this is mine. But I will let you copy it. Do you know how to use the office copier?"

"Yes."

"Good. If you can carefully take it apart and put it back together, go make two copies. One for each of you to read through."

"What do we do then?" Michelle asked.

"Read it," Danielson said, "see what you learn, write down what you think and then try to figure it out.

"Look for answers."

"Answers to what?" Corey asked.

"Answers to whatever you find," the judge said. "It's how we do things. Now go."

They left the office and went to the copy machine. Corey loaded extra paper while Michelle carefully took the file apart. She fed the separated pages to Corey and he made two copies of each one, giving the originals back to Michelle to reorganize.

They did the best they could with the photographs, copying them with the gray-scale, but Michelle didn't want to bother. Too gross, she told Corey. He made the copies anyway.

As the pages piled up, Corey realized they would need some space to look them over.

"Where can we go with these?" he asked.

"I dunno," Michelle said. "I'll go ask."

She gave the rest of the sheets to Corey and went back to the judge's office. As Corey finished with the last ones, she came back.

"He said go downstairs to the break room. No one should be around and he didn't think Mr. Hingstrom would mind."

They finished making copies and put the original back together. As they walked back toward Judge Danielson's office to return it, Annette came in with bags of things she'd purchased during her break.

Corey handed her the file. "Hi, Mom," he said, "Can we borrow a couple of pens and notepads and would you give this back to the judge?"

"I suppose," she said.

"Thanks," Corey said, "We're going down to the break room." He grabbed the pads and pens and the two kids left the office.

Annette put her things down and took the file into Danielson's office. She put it on the desk.

"My son asked me to return this," she said, "but I have no idea what's going on."

"It's the complete file on the body they found," he replied.

"But why are you letting them look at it?"

"Why not? They might learn something and they could also come up with a new angle or piece of information."

"They're smart kids, Annette," the judge continued. "And they're curious. Look at how they got into this thing in the first place."

"I know, sir," Annette said, "but it's an ongoing investigation, isn't it? Is it right to let two twelve-year olds look at an official case file?

"Won't they mess things up for later?"

"Annette," Danielson said, motioning for her to sit down. "It's not an ongoing case. I talked to Chief Blaise and Sheriff Wingate, and they both agree there's nothing more to investigate. The autopsy showed no evidence of foul play, there's no way right now to even confirm the young man's identity and unless someone steps forward with new information, there's nothing more to be done."

"Yes, sir, but..." Annette said.

"Look," Danielson went on, "I know the situation is sad. It's unfortunate the young man, whoever he was, lay up there in the tower for all these years. It would be nice if we could determine what happened or at least identify the body. But we can't. So officially, the matter is closed."

"I understand that, your honor," Annette said, "but why give the file to Corey and Michelle?"

"It gives them something to do," the judge said. "And let's face it Annette, those two are starting to get on everyone's nerves."

"Have they been that bad?" Annette asked quietly.

Danielson just nodded. "We've tried to be understanding, but you and Mrs. Pritchard have those two so tightly grounded and tethered, it's getting hard for everyone to put up with them.

"So maybe this will keep them occupied and out of everyone's hair for a while."

A buzzer sounded.

"That's five minutes. Let's get back to court."

Down in the basement break room, Corey and Michelle spread the papers over their table. Each was reading pages at their own pace and writing some things down as they went. Mostly things they didn't understand like medical terms and long strange words.

"This is harder than I thought," Michelle said.

"I know," Corey replied. "Here's another word I can't get. Sub-cuh… sub-cooten…"

"Subcutaneous, I suspect," said a voice from behind. They looked up to see Judge Barker standing there.

"What are you two reading?" he asked.

"A file," Michelle said. "Judge Danielson said we could."

"It's all the stuff on that guy we found," Corey added.

"Ah, yes," Barker said, joining the kids at the table. "An interesting story. I read through it myself."

"So what are you finding out?" his honor continued.

"Not really much," Michelle said. "A lot of these words are hard to understand."

"I know what you mean, I have trouble with some of those terms too," Barker said. "But I keep a big reference book at my desk to help out. Judge Danielson probably has one too, so ask to borrow it if you need."

"We will, sir," Corey said. "That's why we're writing them down."

"Good," Barker said. "What else are you writing down?"

"Well, I want to know all about him and when he got up there," Corey said, reading from his notes. "And how he fell and what happened after that, and…"

"Me too," Michelle said, "And I want to know if his mom and dad missed him and where they looked, and…"

"Whoa, you two," Barker said. "Those are all good questions. But you've got too many. You need to come up with what the big questions are, then start breaking them down."

"What do you mean?" Corey asked.

"Well, son," the judge said, "when I have to decide a case, and that usually means looking through a lot of stuff like this, I start with three areas. What do I know, what do I need to know, and what does it all mean. That way I can keep it all organized as I look at everything."

"Now usually there's already a great big question I have to answer in a case, so I use these things as a way to get started. You might try the same thing."

"How do you mean?" Michelle asked.

"Think about what you really want to know. What's the big final question you want answered or the main thing you want to find out," the judge replied.

Corey and Michelle thought for several seconds.

"I want to know who the guy really was and what happened to him," Corey said.

"I want to know why he was lost up there and why no one ever looked for him," Michelle added.

"Now *those* are really good questions," Barker said, "and you should write them down. Then you can list everything you learn or find out under one of them. Like an outline."

"Should we start over?" Corey asked.

"Heavens no," Judge Barker said. "Keep going through this stuff and making notes. Figure out what you know and where to start."

"Then what?"

"Then you can begin working on what you need to know."

Judge Barker left the kids with the file and notes.

Two hours went by and they'd made it most of the way through the thick reports. Michelle worked faster since she avoided looking at the photos and understood more of the Latin and scientific words than Corey did. He made more notes on things.

Just before five o'clock, Corey's phone buzzed. He looked at the message.

"It's my mom," he said. "It's time to go home."

"What do we do next?" Michelle asked.

"I'm going to finish reading through this tonight," Corey answered, "and then do what Judge Barker said. I'm going to write down what I know and what I learned from the file."

"Okay," Michelle said, "I will too. We can work some more on this tomorrow."

They gathered up their papers and went back upstairs to meet Mrs. Palmer.

The next morning, once all the courts were in session and the other county functions going strong for the day, Corey and Michelle headed back to the break room with their files and notes. Both had read through most everything and each had a lot of notes and questions.

"We really don't know much, do we?" Corey said.

"Not really," Michelle said, "but we do know he was up there for around fifty years and Doctor Driscoll doesn't think he was murdered or anything."

"Yeah," Corey answered, "and all we really have to go on is that library card."

Michelle sorted through her pages to the copy of the Craigsville library card. "Then let's start from here. What does this tell us?"

Corey took the card copy from his file. "It's labeled *Adult* so he had to be twelve in nineteen sixty-one, so that would mean he was born in…"

"Nineteen forty-nine," Michelle said, doing the math.

"Okay," Corey said, "but if this wasn't his first card, then he could be older."

"You're right," Michelle said, "but the report says he was probably between twelve and fifteen. So it was probably his first adult library card."

"How can we find out?" Corey asked.

Michelle thought for a second. "I could ask my mom. Maybe the library has old records."

"But it won't really prove who he was," Corey said. "We'd need something official for that."

"Yeah, like a birth certificate or something."

Corey thought for a second. "I know, I'll go down to the records office and ask them."

"Won't the police or sheriff's office do that?" Michelle asked.

"They might," Corey replied. "But that doesn't mean we can't. And Judge Danielson did say we should try to find answers.

"I think it will be okay."

"Okay, let's go," Michelle said, "We can meet later to compare notes."

They gathered their things and left. Michelle called her mother as they got to the main floor to say she was on her way to the library. Corey went into the Wagner County Records Office.

Two women were working behind the counter. Corey spoke to the younger one.

"I'm looking for a birth certificate or something on someone born in nineteen forty-nine," he said. "At least I think that's when he was born."

"Is it a relative?" the woman asked.

"No, ma'am," Corey said, "I guess you could say it's research."

"We can't really do that, young man," the woman replied. "You have to have a better reason than just research."

"Well," Corey said, "It's about the dead body they found up in the clock tower."

The older woman looked up. "You mean the dead body *you* found, don't you?"

"Yes, ma'am," Corey said. The older woman came over to join Corey and her colleague.

"It's alright, Martha," she said. "Let him look at the records. His mother works for Judge Danielson and I'm sure there won't be a problem.

"Besides, these are public records."

Martha sighed and went back into the office. In a minute, she returned with a large hard-bound ledger. She put it on the counter.

"Okay, young man," she said. "Here's what we'll do. This is the master record ledger for nineteen forty-nine. Every child born in Wagner County, every marriage, divorce, and death are listed here.

You can look through this to see if you what you're looking for is there. Then we'll see about finding a copy of the official document."

"Yes, ma'am," Corey said. "Do I have to stand here to look through it?"

"That's the way it usually works," Martha said.

"Don't worry," the older woman said, "it won't take that long. I doubt much happened around here back then."

Corey opened the ledger and started searching. The book was divided into record types, so he quickly found the section with birth records. There were several pages and the records were listed chronologically. Everything was handwritten, so he concentrated to read carefully. This slowed him down a little, but the older lady was right. It didn't take very long.

In the middle of the second page, Corey found what he thought he needed. A boy named Phillip Edwin Cooper was born on March 19th. His parents were listed as Arthur Danforth Cooper and Joanne Priscilla Cooper (nee Kaplan).

Corey wrote the information down and continued looking through the rest of the year. He needed to be sure. He found several other Coopers, but no Phillip. This had to be it.

He called to Martha.

"I think this is it," he told her. "Can I get a copy of the actual birth certificate?"

"I suppose," Martha said, "but we normally charge for copies."

"How much?" Corey asked, hoping the three dollars in his pocket would cover it.

"Don't worry," the older woman said. "If you don't have enough, we'll just charge it to Judge Danielson's court."

Martha left to find the document and make the copy. While she was gone, Corey looked through the rest of the ledger. He didn't expect to find anything, but the old book was interesting. *Everything seemed to create a record*, he thought.

He saw some names he recognized, but he didn't really know anyone from this past era.

Martha came back with the copies of Phillip Cooper's birth certificate. She gave Corey a form to fill out and sign and then told him how much.

It ended up being two dollars.

"You know, young man," Martha said, as Corey completed the form. "This is usually police work. Why are you involved?"

"My friend and I are curious," Corey said. "We found the body and we want to know what happened. Judge Danielson said we could."

Martha didn't say any more, and Corey left with the birth certificate.

Over at the library, Michelle was fighting a different battle. Her mother agreed to let her look through old library card records, but no one knew if any existed that far back or where they were stored. One of the other staff members called the oldest person she knew who'd worked there and found out the old card records were stored in the basement in several old file cabinets.

Guided by her mother, Michelle went downstairs to where the cabinets were supposed to be. They were there, alright, but covered in dust and some drawers were almost impossible to open.

"Put everything back where you find it," Mrs. Pritchard said, "and come on back upstairs when you're done."

"Okay, Mom."

Michelle opened the first file drawer and started looking. She scanned the file labels first, hoping to see some organization. This first drawer held overdue records and fine payments. The next drawers held more, with folders labeled for successive years.

She moved to the next cabinet. She couldn't open the top drawer. It was rusted stuck or maybe off its track.

Please don't let it be in there, she prayed silently.

The next drawer did open and looking at the file labels, Michelle realized this could be what she needed. The first folder said, *Library Cards Issued – 1955.*

She looked at the second folder. It said the same thing, so she checked the next several ones. They were in order, though some years had several folders. The last file listed 1960.

Michelle closed the drawer and closed her eyes for a moment. With luck, the next drawer down held the year she needed. Otherwise, 1961 was in the stuck drawer above.

She took a breath and opened the third drawer in the cabinet.

Her luck held. The first folder's label said, *Library Cards Issued – 1960,* but the second listed 1961. So did the next three. She pulled all four out and closed the drawer.

Sitting cross-legged on the basement floor, she opened the top folder and began looking at the records. The card applications seemed to be in a random order. They weren't alphabetical, and Michelle couldn't see any date order either. So she kept looking.

As she checked each form, she noticed some were new cards and some were renewals. Back in those years, everyone needed to fill out the application form each time a card was issued.

She found Phillip Cooper's application in the third folder. It listed his date of birth as March 19, 1949, and showed the card to be good until December 31, 1963.

Remembering the renewal type applications, she went back to the cabinet and found the folders labeled 1964. If Phillip Cooper wasn't the body she and Corey found, he might have renewed his card.

Several minutes later, Michelle finished looking through the later year, but found no record of a renewal for Phillip Cooper.

Putting all the folders back, except the one where she found what she was looking for, Michelle went back upstairs.

"Mom," she said walking up to her mother's desk.

"Shhh," Mrs. Pritchard said sharply. "Library rules."

"Sorry," Michelle whispered. "But I think I found it. Can I make some copies?"

Within minutes, Michelle was outside with her copies and headed back to the courthouse.

She went to the records office first, but Martha told her Corey left a while back. So she headed down to the break room.

Corey looked up from his papers when she sat down.

"I've got something," she said.

"So do I," Corey replied. "I found a birth certificate and I think it's our guy."

"I found the file with his library card information," Michelle said, "and it was never renewed."

"Let me see," Corey said. Michelle gave him a copy of the form.

"Let me see the birth certificate," she said. Corey slid the copied document over to her. They each looked at the new information.

"We might have the answer," Corey said. "The timing works and there's no evidence he lived longer than nineteen sixty-three, and the other reports say he was about fourteen.

"Maybe we've solved it."

"Hold it, Corey," Michelle said. "These give us some more clues, but I don't think it's the answer."

"Remember what the judge said?" she continued, "what do we know, what do we need to know and what does it mean?"

"But I think we can use these to prove the body was Phillip Cooper," Corey said.

"No," Michelle said, "These don't prove it was him just the name is real. We need more."

"Like what?"

"Like something tying things together. Something official. We need to know what really happened and when."

"And if anything was ever reported."

"Like a police report or something?" Corey asked.

"Yes," Michelle said, "that's a great idea. If this Phillip Cooper was trapped up there all this time, maybe somebody reported him missing."

"Do you think the police have records that old?" she asked.

"I don't know," Corey said, "but we can go find out."

As they began putting away all their papers, Corey's phone buzzed. He looked at the text message.

"Court's broken for lunch," he said. "Mom wants us upstairs."

"Good, I'm hungry," Michelle said.

Annette sent the kids over to Hickman's Diner to pick up the order called in earlier. She ordered sandwiches and chips for the kids. As they ate, Corey brought his mother up to date on what they'd found that morning.

"So we figured we go over to the public safety building this afternoon and see if there are any old reports or something about the guy."

"Behave," Annette said. "Don't get into any trouble over there."

"Yes, ma'am," Michelle said.

VIII

Sergeant Bannon sat behind the desk at the Craigsville Police Department. He looked up as the kids entered.

"Can I help you two?" he asked.

"Yes, sir," Corey answered. "We'd like to talk to someone about some old records or files."

"We're doing some research into a person's identity," Michelle added.

Bannon raised his eyebrows and stood up. "You'd need to talk to the chief about that," he said. "I'll see if he's got time."

Bannon walked to an office behind the desk off the large open area. Three officers kept working at their desks.

"Hey, chief," he said through an open door, "got a couple of kids out here asking about old files. You got a minute to talk to them?"

They didn't hear the answer, but Bannon turned to Corey and Michelle and motioned them to come back.

"Come on, you two," he said.

A few seconds later, the kids sat across a desk from Craigsville's Chief of Police.

Robert Blaise looked somewhat like Sheriff Wingate. Both were over six feet tall with broad shoulders and stocky frames. Both men kept their hair closely cropped and both were beginning to fight the middle-age paunch.

Chief Blaise began in law enforcement with the Wagner County Sheriff after retiring from the U.S. Army. He rose to be Wingate's chief deputy and top administrator, and the two men still worked well and easily together.

They were friends too, even though Blaise ran against Wingate for the sheriff's job two elections ago.

"I am going to WHUP you good, boy," Wingate had warned Blaise back then.

"I know," Blaise had replied, *"but come on, Abe. We can't be giving you this job on a pass EVERY time. People need a choice."*

"Besides," he'd continued, *"it will be good practice for when I really run for the job after you retire."*

The sheriff cruised to re-election that year as always.

Blaise might have tried again, but took this job when the previous chief resigned along with about half his department over a corruption investigation. Some officers, including two detectives, went to prison and the chief quit before the city council could fire him. Sheriff Wingate's recommendation tipped the scales for the new chief.

Even with their similar shapes and sizes, no one could doubt which department each ran as Chief Blaise wore the typical police blue uniform, with a light blue shirt over dark blue trousers. Sheriff Wentworth always wore traditional sheriff brown.

The men insisted their officers do likewise. Though they shared functions and cooperated on many things, each felt separate identities were important.

After asking their names and shaking hands, the chief sat back in his chair.

"Alright," he said, "what can I do for you?"

"Well, sir," Corey began, "it's about the body we found up in the courthouse clock tower. Michelle and I are trying to find out what really happened and when."

"We also want to find out if anybody ever looked for him," Michelle said.

"And you think the police might have some records?" Blaise asked.

"Yes, sir," Corey said. "If he was reported missing, there would be a file, wouldn't there?"

Blaise nodded.

"And if there is, maybe it has some details on who the person was and everything, wouldn't it?" Corey continued.

"Don't you even know who he was?" the chief asked.

"We think we do," Michelle said. "We've read the doctor's reports and we've come up with some other things, so we're pretty sure we know who it was."

"We just want to check the files out to see if there's any more information," Corey added.

"Well, kids," the chief said sighing, "I wish I could help you, but the answer is no."

"Why not?" Corey asked.

"Son, you're asking to rumble around and paw through tons of old files, records, and evidence. I can't let that happen."

Chief Blaise leaned forward, resting his elbows on the desk.

"I read the report on that body too," he said, "and while there are some interesting questions about it, there's not enough to justify looking through our old records."

"But we know what we're looking for," Corey said, "and we will be careful."

"Do you really know?" Blaise said. "It seems you might have a name to go with the body, but nothing really ties it together. Besides, there are things like the chain of custody and the statute of limitations.

"Do you know what those mean?"

"Sort of," Michelle said.

"Well then," the chief said, "Let me explain. First of all, even though a lot of the records you want to look at are really old, all of them are official records and case evidence. You might not believe this, but some of those old cases never got solved. So they are still officially under investigation. We can't let outsiders touch them or disrupt how things are tracked and handled officially.

"That's chain of custody."

"But we're looking for something over fifty years ago," Corey said.

"That may be true," Blaise said, "and if this were something like an old robbery or a missing antique, I might let you look. It wouldn't matter anymore. That's what the statute of limitations is; it means after a period of time, something isn't considered a crime anymore.

"The problem is, when somebody's been killed, that limit never runs out."

Blaise stood up. "I'm sorry, you two, but you'll have to look somewhere else."

"Are you looking, sir?" Michelle asked. "Are the police or sheriff's office trying to find out who he was?"

Chief Blaise looked her sternly. "That's none of your concern, young lady."

Corey and Michelle left dejected. Outside, they sat on a bench next to the sidewalk.

"What do we do now?" Michelle said.

"I don't know," Corey said. "I think we're done. I don't know where else to look."

"Well, well, well," they heard from someone in the street, "if it isn't the clock tower twits—I mean twins."

Corey and Michelle looked up at a taller and older boy on a bicycle. Michelle rolled her eyes.

"Stuff it, Cooper," Corey said to the boy.

Tommy Cooper got off his bike and put the kickstand down. He was a year older and three inches taller than Corey. He was also much heavier with a round face and dark hair.

He walked over to Corey and Michelle.

"What are you doing here?" he asked. "Did you find another corpse? What was it this time, a dead bird or maybe a rat? I bet that scared the crap out of you didn't it, Palmer?"

"None of your business, creep," Michelle said.

Tommy leaned close to Michelle. "Why do you hang out with this loser, girl? You're cute enough to hang with me and my friends. Why don't you lose this jackass?" He reached out and stroked Michelle's cheek.

"We can have some real fun."

She swatted Tommy's hand away. "Don't do that," she said.

Corey stood and pushed Tommy away.

"Leave her alone," he said. "Leave both of us alone."

"What are you going to do, Palmer," Tommy said, laughing, "fight me? You want to *defend* the girl's honor?"

He stepped close to Corey with a raised fist. "You want to mix it up, stupid? I'll break you in half."

"You know, if y'all want to fight," said a voice at the building door, "you might want to take it somewhere else."

The kids looked back to see an officer walking toward them.

"Though I will admit, it would be convenient to get my first collar of the day without leaving the office."

The officer walked up to the trio. Her name badge said *Shelton* and Corey recognized her as the officer who climbed back up to the bell to view the body.

After making the trio identify themselves, she asked, "Is there a problem?"

"No, ma'am."

"Not really."

"Good," Officer Shelton said. "Then let's carry on. By the way, whose bike is blocking the sidewalk?"

"Mine," Tommy said.

"Well, Mr. Cooper, I suggest you move it."

As he started toward his bicycle, Tommy spoke quietly to Corey.

"Wait 'til school, Palmer, this isn't over."

Though shaking inside, Corey kept his voice even. "You know, it's too bad the guy we found wasn't your dad. Then you wouldn't exist."

"What are you talking about, dumbass?" Tommy said.

"That guy we found in the clock tower," Corey said, "he was a Cooper. And I guess he was too dumb to get out of there.

"Like you."

Tommy grabbed Corey's shirt with one hand and drew his other back in a fist.

"I thought I told you to move along, Mr. Cooper," Officer Shelton said sternly.

After Tommy pedaled away, Shelton looked at Corey and Michelle.

"You two have anything to say?" she asked. They both shook their heads.

"Alright then," she continued. "Actually, I came out to see what else was going on. I saw you two inside with the chief. What did you want?"

"We wanted to look at some old records," Corey said, "but he wouldn't let us. He said it could mess things up with real cases. Even if they're old ones."

"Yes, that's pretty much the way it works," Shelton said.

"And he acted like the police and sheriff aren't even looking," Michelle said. "That's not fair."

"I wouldn't say that," Officer Shelton replied, "the case—what there is—is actually on my desk. But there's just nothing for the police to investigate."

"That is, unless you have anything," she continued, "it's why I came out. I wanted to ask if you've really found something out."

"We think so," Corey said. He quickly explained about the birth certificate and the library card.

"Interesting," Shelton said, "but I think the chief's right. It's not really enough to justify looking through our old files. You're going to need more."

"But we don't have any place else to look," Michelle said.

"Sure you do," the officer said. "Have you tried the library for other records?"

"My mom works there," Michelle said. "I've looked, but they don't keep files and records on things like this."

"What about the newspaper?" Shelton asked. "They might have old copies and things."

"What are you talking about?" Corey asked.

Shelton just shook her head at the two. "You are showing your age, guys," she said. "You really are too young."

"It's like this," she continued. "Where do you think people looked up information before there were computers? They went to the library, to museums and looked through old books and papers. And they always checked old newspapers for details and first-hand accounts."

"That's where I'd start, if I were you," Shelton said.

"Do you think the *Record / Times* would let us look?" Michelle asked.

"Go over and ask," Officer Shelton replied. "I think they're still open."

Corey and Michelle thanked Shelton and headed off.

For almost a century, the *Craigsville Record / Times* took up the bottom floors of a three-story brick building four blocks off the square. Business offices were upstairs with the newsroom and advertising offices on the ground floor. The presses were in the basement.

Eight years ago, however, the paper built a modern printing plant and office building east of town by the highway. All the printing, distribution, and most of the general business functions moved out there. Reporters and editors stayed downtown in the old building, but knew they'd be moving out to the new place eventually.

An old-fashioned bell tinkled as Corey and Michelle walked into the office. Only one man could be seen, typing away at a computer terminal on one of the desks.

Without looking up, he said, "Sorry folks, we're done for the day. The paper's gone to press and unless it's breaking news, it can wait 'til tomorrow."

"It's about a dead body," Corey said.

"That works," the man said as he moved in a blur. He stood up, grabbed a notebook from the desk and marched toward the front counter where the kids stood.

He stopped short and looked at the two.

"Wait a second," he said. "Aren't you the two youngsters who found that body in the clock tower?"

Corey and Michelle nodded.

"And that's the body you're here about?"

They nodded again.

"That's not breaking news," he said. "In fact, that's so old it's hardly news."

The man tossed his notebook down. "It was barely worth the short page one article we gave it."

"Oh, well," he continued, "since you're here, what can I do for you?"

"We're trying to found out about the body we found," Corey said. "We want to figure out who he really was and what happened to him."

"And we want to see if anyone ever looked for him," Michelle added.

"He was up there a long time," Corey said.

"Yeah," Michelle said. "Why didn't someone find him before we did?"

"What happened?"

"Hold on, you two," the man said, shaking his head after following the back-and-forth. "You've got this routine down pat, don't you?

"Let's start from the beginning, what are your names?"

Corey and Michelle introduced themselves.

"Nice to meet you. I'm Rich Geltsin, Editor-in Chief and general whatever around here. Now what is it you're looking for?"

"Like we said, we're trying to learn the whole story on the dead body we found."

"Alright," Geltsin said, "but first, tell me what you've got. Then maybe we can figure out how I can help." He motioned for them to come around the counter into the office area. They walked to a desk with two chairs next to it.

"Where is everyone?" Michelle asked.

"I told you when you came in," Geltsin said, "We've finished for the day. The paper's being printed out at the new plant, and all the reporters went home for the day."

"What happens if something happens?" Michelle asked.

"We've got phones and we'll figure something out.

"Now, tell me your story," Geltsin said, opening his notebook.

The two kids quickly told the editor about getting trapped and finding the body. They also explained how Judge Danielson let them look at the medical examiner's file and listed the things they'd found since then, like the birth certificate and the library card. They finished with how Chief Blaise wouldn't let them look at the police records.

"Okay," Geltsin said after they finished, "So you need to know more about what happened when the dead person disappeared."

"Yessir."

"And you think we might have some old papers with that type of information?"

The kids nodded.

"Well, you might be right," Geltsin said, "but there's not much to go on. You'd probably have to look through a lot of old issues. Maybe five or six hundred, if we have them all. That's going to be an awful lot of work, and you may not find anything."

"Why that many?" Michelle asked.

"Well, even though the *Record / Times* only comes out during the week, that's still over two hundred issues each year. Based on your story, the dead guy could have disappeared sometime between nineteen sixty-one and nineteen sixty-four. You'd have to look through every one."

"What if we could narrow it down?" Corey asked.

"That would help," Geltsin said, "but how could you do that?"

Corey pulled out his thin wallet. He opened it and took out two one-dollar bills.

"I found these on the body," he said, laying them on the desk. The folded paper he'd found slipped from between them.

"Corey!" Michelle said, loudly. "I don't believe this! You shouldn't have done that. It's evidence!"

"I know," Corey said, "but I stuffed them in my pocket and forgot about them. I found them later after we got home that morning."

"Why didn't you turn them in later?" Michelle asked.

"I guess I didn't want to get in more trouble," Corey replied. "Things were bad enough."

He turned to Geltsin. "Am I going to get in trouble?"

"Not from me," Geltsin said. "I'm not a cop."

He picked up the bills and looked them over.

"So how does this narrow things?" he asked.

Corey took the bills back. "This one says *Series 1963A*. The guy couldn't have had it if he was trapped before then."

"That is a good point," Geltsin said, "and it's a clue. We can look to see when these were printed and that will narrow down the time frame."

He noticed the folded paper.

"What's this?" he asked. "Something else you found?"

"Just a number, we don't have any idea what it means," Corey said.

Geltsin opened the torn sheet and looked at the number. Then he laid it aside.

"We can worry about this later," he said, "but on the whole, I think I can help. You'll have to do most of the work, though." He took the bills from Corey.

"Here's what we'll do. I want to make a copy of these, and I'll look up when they were printed. You two can come back in the morning and we'll go to the morgue."

"NO!" Michelle said, shrinking back into her chair. "I don't want to go there. We saw the body, why do we have to go to the morgue?"

Corey didn't say anything, but he shrank back, too.

Geltsin laughed. "Take it easy, it's not what you think. The morgue is what a newspaper calls where it stores back issues, old photos, files, and notes and things.

"There aren't any bodies."

"Why do you call it that?" Corey asked after settling down.

"I have no idea," Geltsin said, "but that's been the term for a long time."

"Anyway," he continued, "our morgue is down in the basement, where we used to have the presses. So wear some old clothes, because you will get dirty."

"What time?" Corey asked.

"How about nine o'clock," Geltsin said. Corey and Michelle nodded.

"And one more thing," Geltsin continued. "See if I can get a look at that file, too. Who knows? There might be a real story here.

"Oh, and don't spend those bills, young man, they might be important. At least they'll be nice souvenirs."

"I won't," Corey said.

The kids left the paper and went back to the courthouse to meet Annette.

Geltsin knew there was a story one way or another. If the kids did find out who the dead boy was and what really happened, he'd have something the entire state would enjoy. If not, he still had the story of the two youngsters getting trapped and then trying to find out about the corpse. That might only interest people in Wagner County, but it would still be a good story.

And lots of fun to write.

Richard Geltsin didn't do much writing these days. As editor-in-chief and basically top dog, he spent almost all his time running things both here and out at the new building.

He didn't really own the *Record / Times* because his mother still held title to the paper and owned all the shares of the business. Vivian Schneider hadn't worked at the paper since before Richard's father passed away. Now remarried, she and her second husband spent most of their time in a large RV travelling the country. They drove and hiked through national parks and forests, visited historic sites throughout and only came back to Wagner County occasionally.

IX

The next morning, Corey and Michelle drove their mothers nuts as they tried to hurry things along and get over to the newspaper office. Corey tried to explain why he dressed in old clothes, but Annette missed most of it.

Over at the Pritchard home, Michelle wolfed down her breakfast and cleared the dishes before Marybelle asked. Then she kept hurrying her mother along.

"Come on, Mom," Michelle said, "We have to get going. I need to meet Corey so we can get over to the paper by nine o'clock."

As they drove into town, Marybelle called Annette.

"What is going on with these two?" she asked her friend.

"I have no idea, Marybelle," Annette replied, "but they're into something. You'd think we lifted their punishment."

"And what's this about the *Record / Times*?" Marybelle asked.

"Corey says they're going to look through some old issues."

"Is that why Michelle looks like she's homeless?"

Annette laughed. "You should see Corey. He looks like a bum begging for money."

The kids would have asked to be dropped at the paper, but needed to get some notes from the box of stuff they usually left in the judge's office. After grabbing what they needed, along with pens and notepads, they walked over to the *Record / Times*.

They walked in two minutes before nine.

Rich Geltsin sat on a desk with half a dozen people around him.

"That's a plan, people," he said. "Let's get going. We can get everything in for Monday by this afternoon and set the front page on Sunday like normal."

"Check in if you need, but call my cell. I'm working on something special this morning."

As the group split up, Geltsin called one of the reporters. "Hey, Boyd," he said, "do you really think the Warriors will be that good this season?"

"You should see the new kid they've got playing quarterback," the other man replied.

"Yeah, but beating Cherokee County *and* Titusville?"

"Who knows, boss?"

Two of the people headed toward where Corey and Michelle stood.

"Hey, kids," one said, "What you need?"

Geltsin looked up. "It's okay; they're here to see me."

The other person turned back to the editor. "What's going on? You chasing stories again, chief?"

"Maybe," Geltsin said. "It's none of your business. Now get going."

The reporters left, chuckling.

Geltsin motioned for Corey and Michelle to come around the counter into the office area.

"Mornin'," he said. "You two look like you're ready to get dirty and look through some old stuff."

"We are," Michelle said.

"Alright," Geltsin said, "Let's go. We're going downstairs."

He led them to a door halfway down the back hallway. Opening it, he flipped a light switch.

"The basement's pretty big," he said as they went down, "but there are lots of racks and file cabinets. Watch your step."

At the bottom, Geltsin turned on more lights and the kids saw the newspaper's morgue.

"It looks like a warehouse," Corey said.

"It's really what it is," Geltsin said. "We store all our back issues, old files, notes, photographs, and things like that."

"Why?" Michelle asked.

"So we have a record of things," Geltsin said. "Kind of like why you're here."

"How old is all this stuff?" Corey asked.

"We've got just about every issue of the paper since the nineteen twenties," Geltsin said, "That's when the two papers merged. Before that, we've got most of the old *Craigsville Record* but not many of the old *Times.*"

"Does anybody ever come look at this?" Michelle asked.

"We've had some college professors look through old papers for their research," Geltsin answered, "and sometimes folks want to look up old relatives.

"But I think you're the first who wanted to identify a dead body."

They walked down the center aisle to a table set up with chairs.

"You can look through things here," Geltsin said, "but first we'll go grab the issues to start with."

Geltsin took some folded sheets from his pocket.

"That reminds me. I looked up your dollars, Corey, and you were right. The newer one didn't become available until late 1963. So I think you should start with July and August that year and work forward."

"How far?" Michelle asked.

"Who knows?" Geltsin said. "We'll have to see. Now let's go grab the papers."

Geltsin led them through the rows of racks and file cabinets, checking labels as he went. Four rows over from the center, they came to the year they wanted. Geltsin pulled a large bound volume from the shelf.

"This is all the front pages from the second half of 1963," he said, handing the book to Michelle. "I doubt you'll find anything on them, but it's a start.

"Let's get to it."

Old issues were packed in labeled boxed, two months worth in each. They weren't large, but were quite heavy. Geltsin pulled the boxes with papers from July of '63 through February of 1964. He doubted either of the kids could carry one and he didn't want to make four trips.

He went to find a two-wheeled dolly to haul the boxes.

Back at the table, they placed the first two boxes on the table with the front-page volume. Geltsin opened the first box and removed all the old issues.

"Okay," he said, "this is where you get to do the hard part. Look through every issue for something about your dead body. You have a name and an estimated age."

"Do we have to look through every page?" Corey asked.

"Probably not," Geltsin replied. "The paper's been organized the same way for years. The back section is mostly sports, classifieds, obituaries, and ads. Most of the news is in the front section. Concentrate on that."

"Okay," Michelle said.

"I'll be upstairs if you need me," Geltsin said. "Let me know if you find anything or need help."

"Thanks, Mr. Geltsin," Corey said. The editor left.

Corey took the first issue for July and gave the second one to Michelle.

"We should probably write down each date we look at as we go," she said.

Corey agreed and they started looking through the old pages.

An hour later, they'd made it through September and about half of October. Their hands were colored black with rubbed-off newsprint and both kids were beginning to sweat in the summer heat. The basement was cooler than upstairs, but not air-conditioned.

"I need a break," Corey said, "It's really hot down here."

"Me too," Michelle said.

They marked their progress and went upstairs. Geltsin and a woman were talking at one of the desks when they entered the main office area.

"Find something?" Geltsin asked, looking at them.

"No," Michelle said, "we're just taking a break. It's hot down there."

Geltsin laughed. "You should have worked here when the presses were running there."

"Anyway," he continued, "if you've got some change, there's a soda machine in the back."

The kids bought sodas and went back downstairs.

Back at their work table, they finished October without finding anything about Phillip Cooper or any missing children.

"Want to split these differently?" Corey asked as he removed the papers for November and December.

"How?" Michelle asked.

"How about I take November and you take December?"

"Okay, but how will that help?"

"It just mixes things up a little."

Michelle shrugged and Corey passed the stack of December issues to her. They flipped pages silently.

Twenty minutes later, Corey reached over and nudged Michelle.

"I think I've got something," he said. "Look at this." He passed the open section over.

On page four of a Friday issue from late November was a small article with the headline, *"Local Boy Missing."*

Michelle read the whole article:

Local Boy Missing

Police are looking for any information on the whereabouts of Phillip E. Cooper, 14, of Craigsville.

The youth was last seen on Wednesday leaving Craigsville High School at the end of the day. He was reported missing to the police on Thursday, by his father.

Young Mr. Cooper is the son of Mr. and Mrs. Arthur D. Cooper, 814 Woodlawn Drive, Craigsville. He is described as five feet tall with light brown hair and wearing a checked shirt and dungarees.

Anyone who has seen Phillip is asked to contact the Craigsville Police Department at JL5-6161.

"Wow," Michelle said, "this is something. And that name's familiar."

"Which name?"

"Arthur Cooper. I think I saw it in December."

She started looking back through the later month's issues. Corey set the paper with the small story aside and kept looking through the remaining November papers.

A few minutes later, Michelle found the story she'd seen earlier.

"Here it is," she said, "from early December. Arthur Cooper was killed and this is the story on his funeral."

"Yeah, and I found the connection," Corey said. "Here's a story from later in November about a wreck out on a county road."

They traded papers and read what each discovered.

Accident Claims Prominent Local Citizen

An accident late Saturday night claimed the life of Arthur D. Cooper, 39 of Craigsville. The accident occurred several miles outside the city on the two-lane paved road called Redland Farm Road.

The Wagner County Sheriff's office stated no other vehicles were involved and no one else was injured.

The damaged car was reported by another motorist who saw the vehicle resting against a tree several yards off the road. He called the Sheriff's office after driving into town.

Officers were dispatched and discovered Mr. Cooper still inside the damaged car. An ambulance arrived soon after but Mr. Cooper was declared dead at the scene.

No cause for the accident has been determined but Deputy Joseph Collier stated a full investigation will take several days.

Mr. Cooper is survived by his wife, Joanne, though it is reported the couple had begun divorce proceedings. The couple also have a son, Phillip, age 14.

Arthur Cooper Laid to Rest

Mr. Arthur Danforth Cooper was laid to rest today after funeral services at Second Presbyterian Church in Craigsville. The service was presided over by the Reverend Lawrence Morton.

The funeral featured hymns by the church choir and a reading from the Old Testament book of Psalms. Reverend Morton delivered the only Eulogy.

Mr. Cooper was a prominent member of the Cooper family, being the son of Clayton Roberts Cooper and the nephew of Thaddeus Cooper. He was active in the family's business ventures as a co-owner of the Cooper Millworks Company and also part of the Ryerson-Cooper Farms Company.

Members of the Cooper family attended the services including his mother, sister and several cousins.

Mr. Cooper is reported to have been separated from his wife, Joanne, at the time of his death. Mrs. Cooper did not attend the funeral.

Mr. Cooper was later interred at Eden Valley Cemetery in the Cooper family plot.

"Nothing more about Phillip Cooper," Michelle said.

"I know," Corey replied, "but still, I think we've got something. At least we know exactly when it happened."

"Yeah, but maybe there's more." Michelle lifted the last box onto the table.

"Let's check through January and February of the next year to see if anything else happened."

"Okay. You want January or February?"

At eleven thirty, the kids put the last two months of back issues into their box. They hadn't found anything else about Phillip Cooper or his parents.

They took the issues with their finds upstairs to make copies. Rich Geltsin wasn't around, but a woman working at a computer told them he'd be back soon.

"He ran over to city hall to ask the mayor some questions," she said. "But he told me to keep tabs on you two."

"We found some stories we'd like to get copied," Corey told her.

"Sure," the woman said. "Let's see what you got."

They showed her the three old newspapers and the stories they wanted copied.

"It should work, but the pages will still be pretty big. I'll shrink them as much as I can but still keep them readable."

"Can you make several copies of each?" Michelle asked.

"Not a problem," the woman said. "And I was told to make an extra for Mr. Geltsin. He wanted to see what you found."

In a few minutes, they were on their way back to the courthouse.

Corey and Michelle walked into a flurry of activity in Judge Danielson's office. Everyone was catching up on paperwork and finishing things for the week, since there were no trials scheduled until next week. The judge was eating a sandwich at his desk while reading reports.

Annette looked up as the kids approached her desk.

"Good lord, you two are a mess," she said. "What were you doing, digging through a trash pile?"

"No, Mom," Corey said. "Digging through old newspapers. And we think we found some more information."

Judge Danielson came out of his office.

"What did you find?" he asked.

They unfolded the large copied pages and spread them out on Annette's desk.

"We found some stories about Phillip Cooper and his father," Michelle said.

"And we think we know when it happened," Corey added.

As Judge Danielson and Mrs. Palmer read the short articles, the phone rang. Without thinking, Annette reached over and answered the phone on speaker.

"Judge Danielson's chambers, Annette Palmer speaking."

"Afternoon, this is Rich Geltsin over at the *Record / Times.* Is hizzoner around?"

"Yes, he is," Annette replied. "May I ask what this is about?"

"Two things," Geltsin said. "First one's a file I'm supposed to get a look at."

Annette looked at the judge and shrugged.

"This is Judge Danielson, Mr. Geltsin. May I ask what file you are referring to?"

"The one on the clock tower body," Geltsin said. "I had a deal with those kids looking into it. If I let them look through back issues, they said they'd get me a copy of the full report on the body."

Danielson looked at Corey and Michelle with raised eyebrows. Michelle looked down at the floor. Corey looked away.

The judge smiled. "Well sir, that may be, but I'm not sure. There are some legal and privacy concerns and…"

"Oh come on, Judge," Geltsin cut in. "It's public record anyway and there's freedom of the press and all. Besides, you've already let two youngsters look at it. How's that not violating any of those concerns?"

Now Danielson laughed. "Your point is taken. I can send you a copy."

"But it might be quicker if you just asked Doc Driscoll," the judge continued.

"Will you issue an order to that effect?" Geltsin asked.

"Just tell her I said it's okay," the judge said. "We don't need to be so formal."

"I don't think so, Your Honor," Geltsin replied. "You know how she is about sticking to the rules."

"Alright then," Danielson said, "If she won't give you a copy, ask Sheriff Wingate or Chief Blaise for it.

"Tell them the same thing and give me a call if they give you any problems."

"Better yet," Danielson continued after a beat, "tell them to call Judge Barker. He loves coming down on those two."

"I'll do that," Geltsin said, "Now about the second thing—"

"Before you get to that," Danielson said, "can I ask what you want the file for?"

"Well, Your Honor, based on what I've heard and what those kids found, there just might be a story here. At least I'd like to dig around to see."

"Now the second thing," Geltsin continued, "have you got those two star researchers over there?"

"Uh, yessir," Corey said, "we're both here."

"Alright. Now look, you two did a great job finding this stuff and I hope you find more. I'll even help if I can. But you have to promise me one thing."

"What's that?" Michelle asked.

"Do you know what an exclusive is?" Geltsin asked.

"Yes," Michelle answered, "sort of."

"Good. I want this to be my exclusive. Don't go telling anyone else about it, okay?"

The kids looked at the adults. Judge Danielson nodded.

"Okay," Corey said.

"There's one more thing," Geltsin said. "Remember those other pieces of information you gave me?"

"Uh-huh," Michelle said.

"Well I've got something on them too," Geltsin said. "When can we talk about it?"

Corey looked at his mother, who shook her head.

"I guess we can't do it today," he said.

"That's okay, I'm headed home anyway. How about Monday morning?"

Annette nodded and Corey told the editor they'd be there at nine o'clock. Geltsin said goodbye and hung up.

"You're stating to make waves," the judge said.

"Is it okay?" Michelle asked.

"Lord, yes," Danielson said, "It's getting interesting. What are you going to do next?"

Corey looked at Michelle.

"We don't know," he said. "We've found a lot out, but don't know where to go next."

"Well," Mrs. Palmer said, "you've got some new names. Why not find out more about them?"

"You mean the parents?" Michelle asked.

"Yes," Annette said. "Find out more about Mr. and Mrs. Cooper. That might tell you more about Phillip."

"But who would we talk to?" Corey asked. "We don't know any of the Coopers."

"Everyone knows the Coopers, son," Danielson said. "There must be somebody in that family you can ask."

"Not really," Corey said. "The only one I know is Tommy Cooper, and I don't think he'd talk to me."

"Yeah," Michelle said, "and he's a creep, too. He tried touching me the other day."

They told the judge and Annette about their run-in with Tommy Cooper earlier in the week. They also explained how Officer Shelton broke it up.

"I see your problem," Danielson said. He thought for a few seconds.

"Annette," he said, "would we know of anyone these two might talk to?'

"Well sir, the only Cooper we've dealt with recently is that crazy girl from last year."

"Ah, yes," Danielson said, "Miss Josie. We could certainly ask her. If you'll pull her record, I'll call and ask her to come by."

"In the meantime," he continued, turning to Corey and Michelle, "you two should go get cleaned up and grab some lunch. Then be back here by two-thirty.

"Annette, if you need to take them, go ahead."

"I need to finish these filings, Judge," Annette said.

"I'll have Lucy start on them after she finishes the transcripts. We'll get them done."

While Annette took the kids home to shower, change and eat, Judge Danielson made a phone call. He set up the appointment, but had to put up with a slightly absurd conversation to get it.

X

Annette, Corey and Michelle were back in the office by two o'clock. They'd stopped at the library to tell Marybelle what was happening.

At two-thirty on the dot, nineteen-year-old Josephine Cooper strode into the office and made a beeline for Judge Danielson's open door. She wore tattered low-rise jeans and a tight tank top. Over this she wore a loose open shirt. Her shoes were Chuck Taylor All-Stars and her light brown hair was cut short on the sides with the top gelled into spikes.

"Excuse me, Miss Cooper," Annette said as Josie walked by her desk, "you can't just barge in."

"Sure I can," Josie said. "He's expecting me."

"It's alright, Annette," Danielson said from his desk. "You come on in too, and bring the kids."

Corey and Michelle followed Josie and Annette into the office. Josie slouched in one of the chairs opposite Danielson. Annette sat in the other and the kids stood behind her.

"Why'd you call me down here, Judge?" she asked. "I'm not in trouble again, am I?

"I swear I've been good."

"I'm not aware of anything, Miss Cooper," Danielson said, "but then again, what have you been up to recently?"

"I don't have to say," Josie replied. Judge Danielson laughed.

"Actually, Miss Cooper, I asked you here to meet some people and to ask a favor." He pointed to Corey and Michelle.

"Kids, this is Josephine Cooper," he said. "Miss Cooper, meet Corey Palmer and Michelle Pritchard."

"Hey," Josie said. "So what's this about?"

"You've probably heard about the body found up in the clock tower," Danielson said.

"Sure," Josie said. "Everybody has."

"Well," Danielson continued, "it turns out the person might be a relative of yours."

Josie sat up straight.

"No way!" she said. "You're kidding me!"

"No, we're not," Danielson said. "Everything we've found point to the dead person being named Phillip E. Cooper."

"Never heard of him," Josie said.

"Not surprising," Danielson said. "The body was up there for over fifty years. Before all of our times."

"Kids," the judge continued, "why don't you explain what you've found out about the person in question."

Corey and Michelle quickly explained how they found the body, what they learned from the autopsy and other reports, and what they'd learned from the records office, the library and the newspaper.

"Sounds boring," Josie said after they finished. "And what does it have to do with me, anyway? It was a long time ago."

"Well, Miss Cooper," Danielson said, "we were hoping you might know of someone in your vast family who had some more information about what happened back then. An older relative, perhaps."

Josie closed her eyes for a few seconds to think.

"Aunt Ethel might know," she said, opening her eyes. "She's in her eighties and might remember something from back then."

"Could we talk to her?" Corey asked. "Could you ask her for us?"

"I guess," Josie said. "She might talk if she's in good shape. She doesn't get out much, and she is getting up there."

"When could we go?" Michelle asked.

"Hold your horses," Josie said. "I don't even know if she'd see you. The old girl has her set ways.

"Then again, I'm supposed to go up there for tea this Sunday, so I suppose you could tag along."

"Cool," Corey said. "Can we go, Mom?"

"I don't know," Annette said. "I'm not sure I want you disturbing an elderly woman."

"I wouldn't worry about that," Josie said. "The old girl's pretty hard to rattle, and she's got someone watching out for her, too."

"Let them go, Annette," Danielson said. "I'm sure Miss Cooper will take care of them, and I suspect it will be interesting. If Ethel Cooper is anything like others in that family I've met, she should be quite the character."

"Am I right?" he said to Josie.

"That's one way of putting it," she muttered.

"Alright then," Annette said, "I'll have to check with Mrs. Pritchard, but if she approves, where should I bring them?"

"Where do y'all go to church?' Josie asked.

"Hidden Oaks," Annette said. "Why?"

"I'll meet you there right after the service," Josie said. "It'll make things easier."

"But we need to get home first," Annette said.

"No you don't," Josie said. "The church is on the way, and these two will need to still be in their good clothes anyway."

"Why?" Corey asked.

"Because Aunt Ethel requires her guests to dress properly for Sunday tea," Josie said with a snobbish accent.

"Even I have to dress up."

"Then it's set," Danielson said. "I hope you all have fun." Everyone left the office. Josie was last and as she got to the door, Danielson spoke again.

"Miss Cooper," he said. She turned around.

"Thank you. It's very nice of you to help."

"Don't sweat it, Judge," Josie replied. "It'll probably be more fun than my usual visits with the old bat."

Sunday morning services let out around Noon, and Annette, Corey and Michelle left the church and walked to the parking lot. Josie Cooper leaned against the driver's door of a light blue 1970 Dodge Polara convertible.

"Whoa!" Corey said as they walked up. "Cool car!"

"Behave yourself in it, kid," Josie said. "It's my Daddy's pride and joy."

"How come he let you drive it?" Michelle asked.

"Because we're going up the hill," Josie answered, "and the old lady gets a kick out of seeing it."

"I must say, it makes for a fine entrance," Annette said.

"It does look good, doesn't it?" Josie said. "You would not *believe* the whistles and honks I get when I'm driving it."

"I think I would," Annette said, smiling, "And it's probably not just the car.

"You look very nice today, too, Miss Cooper."

"Why thank you, ma'am," Josie said, blushing a bit. She wore a light yellow sun dress held up by spaghetti straps along with high-heeled white strapped sandals. Her short hair was un-spiked and she even wore a bit of make-up.

Josie opened her door and called to the kids.

"Let's go," she said. "Tea time awaits."

Michelle called shotgun and ran around to the passenger door. Corey climbed into the back seat, claiming the front for the return trip. They found their safety belts on the massive bench seats and fastened them.

"No shoulder belts?" Michelle asked.

"No air bags either," Josie said, "thing is almost as old as my dad."

With the warm summer air whipping through the car, they drove from the church, heading away from town and toward hills to the west. Josie kept the car just around the posted limit on the two-lane road.

Corey leaned on the back of the front seat to be part of any conversation.

A mile into the drive, Josie spoke.

"Okay, you guys," she said. "There are some things I need to tell you before we get to Aunt Ethel's house."

"Is she really your aunt?" Michelle asked.

"My great-aunt," Josie said, "My grandma and her husband were brother and sister."

Michelle did quick calculations in her head. "But your last name is Cooper too," she said, "How's that?"

"That is another long story," Josie said, "and I'm not telling it. Now as I was saying—"

"Why are you really doing this?' Michelle interrupted.

"What? Visiting the old lady?" Josie asked. Michelle nodded.

"My mama wants me to stay in touch with her. Keep the family connection and all that."

"Does your mother visit, too?" Corey asked from the back seat.

"No," Josie said, "they don't like each other at all."

"So how come your aunt likes you?" Corey asked.

"She thinks I'm from another branch of the family," Josie said, tilting her head back toward Corey. "And don't you dare rat me out."

Corey slunk back.

"Now listen, you two," Josie said again.

"You didn't answer my question," Michelle cut in. "Why are you doing *this*? Why are you bringing us along?"

Josie turned partially toward Michelle.

"Girl," she said, "you just don't quit, do you?" Michelle looked down at the car's floor.

"Alright," Josie continued, "If I answer that, will you let me tell you what I need to?"

The kids replied yes.

"Okay then. What I told Judge Danielson was it might be more fun than my usual visits. And I think it will be."

"But the truth is," Josie continued, "I owe the judge a favor. Last year, he did a good thing for me."

"What happened?" Corey asked from the back seat.

"Do you remember that big crazy party out at the lake last month?" Josie said. "The one where all those kids got arrested?"

"Sure," Corey replied. "My mom worked on all the cases with Judge Danielson. She had to stay late some nights."

"You weren't part of that, were you?" Michelle asked.

"No," Josie replied, "but a little over a year ago, some friends and I did something kind of like that. Except we ended up wrecking some yards and houses, and a few parked cars. I got arrested and came up before the judge."

"Did he send you to jail?" Corey asked.

"He could have," Josie said, "but he didn't. He also could have let my parents and my trustees pay for the damage and let it go. But he didn't do that either."

"What did he do?" Michelle asked.

"Made me fix the problems I caused," Josie said. "Judge Danielson sentenced me to put everything right by repairing all the houses and cars I wrecked."

"I spent months working with carpenters and repairmen on it," Josie continued. "Worked hard, too, and learned something."

"What was that?" Michelle asked.

"Doing something is better than doing nothing. And it was kind of fun. But don't tell the judge I said so."

"Anyway," Josie continued, "after I finished the work, Judge Danielson gave me my license back and sealed everything so I won't have a record. So I feel like I owe him and this helps even things up."

They rode in silence for another few minutes.

"Okay, here's how this is gonna work," Josie said, as she made another turn. "First off, Aunt Ethel will probably ask you about yourselves and your families. And she'll also serve you real tea. Well, she might actually give you lemonade, since you're so young and it's summer and all.

"So be polite and answer her questions."

"She'll also offer these cookies," Josie continued. "They're these old fashioned shortbread things like they have in England. They aren't very good, but nibble on them anyway."

"When can we ask her about the dead body?" Michelle asked.

"I wouldn't say it like that," Josie said, "but she'll let you know when she's ready to talk."

"Are we clear?" Josie asked.

"Yes, ma'am," both kids replied.

They drove two more miles in silence.

"Can I ask another question?" Corey said.

"I guess," Josie said.

"Why did you say we're going up the hill?"

"Wait 'til you see."

XI

At one time, the Cooper family owned most of the land making up Wagner and the surrounding counties. They still owned a lot of land today, but sold off most over the past century.

Most of the old holdings were farms and plantations in the early days, and the Coopers built several grand houses in the area. While only one part of the family's holdings still operated as a working farm, the houses survived with some land and different Coopers still owned and lived in them.

Hilltop House was one. Perched on a steep bluff called Brown's Hill, the house stood majestically over the surrounding fields. Originally built for Thaddeus Cooper, it passed to his nephew Clayton. Ethel Cooper was the last member of that branch.

Josie turned off the road onto the Hilltop House driveway. Brick and stone pillars marked the entrance with the house's name arched across the drive in wrought iron. As soon as the car passed under, the grade rose enough to push drivers and passengers back in their seats.

Josie gunned the big Dodge engine up the incline.

"Now you see why it's up the hill?" she asked Corey.

At the top, Josie drove onto the circular end of the driveway and parked the car. Everyone got out and walked up to the front door. Before they climbed the steps to the large wrap-around front porch, a middle-aged African-American woman opened the front door.

"Good afternoon, Josephine," the woman said.

"Afternoon, Lela," Josie replied. "How's Aunt Ethel?"

"Miss Ethel is doing well, and she's expecting you."

They walked into the foyer and Lela closed the door.

"May I ask who you've brought with you?" Lela said.

"This is Corey and Michelle," Josie replied. "I told you about them when I called. They want to ask Aunt Ethel about something from a long time ago."

"Well, come on back," Lela said, moving away from them. "Miss Ethel's on the sun porch."

""Who is that?" Corey asked Josie quietly as they walked.

"Her name's Lela. She takes care of Aunt Ethel," Josie said. "She's like a nurse, cook, maid, and helper rolled into one."

They walked down the central hallway, past a staircase and through a large open back part of the house. Here was a more casual living area with an open kitchen to the left. The sun porch lay beyond, through an open sliding door.

Ethel Cooper sat on the porch in a padded wicker chair. An end-table sat between her and a matching chair. A low coffee table was in front and a cushioned love seat sat opposite.

Josie took the chair next to her great-aunt and the kids sat on the love seat. Michelle put her notebook in between them.

Lela hovered at the sliding door.

"Hello, dear," Ethel said to Josie. "How are you today?"

"Fine, Aunt Ethel, how are you doing?"

"Oh, I'm getting by," the older woman replied, "as well as can be expected."

At eighty-seven years old, Ethel Cooper was doing reasonably well. Thin for her entire life, she looked frail in her later years, but was still strong enough to walk around wherever she needed, except to get up and down the hill. Her eyesight and hearing were beginning to fail, so she couldn't drive herself anymore, nor see well enough to do her shopping or cooking.

After suffering a heart attack four years previously, the doctor put her on some medicine to regulate her heartbeat, and recommended getting some help. So, Ethel hired Lela to help out and take care of her.

"And how are your parents, Josephine, are they well? Miss Ethel asked.

"They're fine," Josie replied, "they send their best."

"That's wonderful, dear, you give them my best, too." Ethel looked over at Corey and Michelle.

"Well now," she said "Who are your young friends?"

"I'm Corey Palmer."

"I'm Michelle Pritchard."

"Yes, indeed," Ethel said. "Now I don't believe we've met before, so if I may, what does your father do, young man?"

"My father's dead," Corey said quietly. "He was killed in Iraq."

"Oh, I'm so sorry," Ethel replied. She looked at Michelle.

"And what about you, young lady, what does your family do?"

"My daddy drives a truck and my mom works at the library."

"Well, that's very nice," Ethel said. "Good honest work. Lela, could you serve now please?"

"I hope you don't mind," she continued. "I know this is supposed to be afternoon tea, but it is so blessedly hot today. So I've asked for lemonade instead."

Lela brought a large tray with four filled glasses and a pitcher of lemonade. She set the tray on the low table, gave glasses to everyone, and placed the pitcher and a tray of shortbread cookies in the table's center.

"You must also try these wonderful things," Ethel said, taking two cookies, "they are just like the ones served in the finest English manor houses."

Corey and Michelle each took one and tasted them.

Josie was right, Corey thought, they weren't very good. But the lemonade was great.

"Now then," Ethel said, "my young niece tells me you wish to ask about something from long ago."

"Yes, ma'am," Corey said. "It's about members of your family from about fifty years ago. Right, Shel?"

"Uh-huh," Michelle said, "we're trying to learn about some people named Cooper who were around way back in the early nineteen sixties."

"We're trying to learn what happened to them," Corey said.

"And who would that be?" Ethel asked.

"Arthur Cooper and his wife, Joanne," Michelle said.

"And their son, Phillip," Corey added.

The old woman froze. Her mouth became set, though after a few seconds, her jaw began to tremble slightly. A tear formed in each eye and ran down her cheeks.

She brought her hand to her mouth, pressing a knuckle against her lips.

Watching from the doorway, Lela saw Miss Ethel's reaction and quickly came into the sun room.

"Now look what you've done. You've upset her," she said.

"What did you say to her, Josephine?" Lela asked sternly.

"I didn't say anything," Josie said. "Aunt Ethel was talking to those two."

Lela turned to Corey and Michelle. "Then I think you'd better leave now. You've distressed my lady."

Ethel took her hand away and took a deep breath.

"No, Lela, it's alright," Ethel said. "They just brought up something I hadn't thought about in many years. I'm sure they didn't mean anything by it."

Ethel used a napkin to dry the tears.

"I'm sorry, young people," she said, "but I hadn't heard poor Arthur's name in a very long time. It's a bit of a shock."

"Yes, ma'am" Michelle said, "We're sorry."

"No, it's alright," Ethel said, "I'm sure you have good reason."

Miss Ethel took some more seconds to compose herself.

"May I ask what that reason is?" she said.

Corey and Michelle looked at each other. Neither wanted to tell the old woman about their discovery. Finally Corey spoke.

"We think we found Phillip Cooper," he said. "At least we found a body that could be him."

Ethel gasped and brought her hand to her mouth again.

"Oh my Lord in Heaven," she said. "Are you sure?"

"Pretty sure," Michelle said. "That's why we're here. We wanted to learn more about him and his parents. We're trying to figure out what really happened to him."

They explained how they'd found the body up in the clock tower and told Miss Ethel what else they'd found.

"My, oh my," Ethel said. "After all this time, to think that boy got trapped up there."

"Yes ma'am," Corey said. "So can you tell us what happened back then?"

"Well, young man," Ethel replied, "I can tell you what I heard. But I wasn't living here then."

Josie Cooper was sitting back in her chair, sipping lemonade, but she sat up and leaned in as Miss Ethel told her story.

"You see, my husband, Robert and I—God rest his soul—were living in Carolina then," Ethel began. "He'd decided to make his own way in the world, rather than join the Cooper family business. We didn't move back here until years after.

"Arthur Cooper was Robert's cousin. He was Mr. Clayton Cooper's son and grew up right here at Hilltop. And like most young men back then, he went off to fight in the war."

"Which war?" Corey asked.

"Why, the Second World War," Ethel said.

"He came back from Europe with Joanne after the war," she continued. "They'd met and got married over there, but she was an American girl. From up north somewhere, I believe, I'm not sure."

Ethel looked at Josie.

"I wouldn't know, Aunt Ethel," Josie said. "This is all new to me."

"Of course, dear," Ethel said. "This was before your time."

"Now as I said, I didn't live here at the time. But I did keep in contact with the family. I do believe in that." Ethel paused to drink some lemonade.

"And so I heard about most everything that happened with those two."

"Arthur Cooper was a very hard-working man," Ethel said, "and he spent long hours at the mill and other Cooper enterprises. His wife kept their home, but really never fit in with our family, and I was told she didn't like Wagner County at all.

"They had Phillip a few years after coming back, and everything should have worked out very well for them."

Michelle opened her notebook and started writing things down. She knew she'd never remember everything Miss Ethel told them.

"Now I really don't like to speak ill of people," Ethel went on, "but both Arthur and Joanne apparently liked to imbibe a bit too much."

"What do you mean?" Corey asked.

"She means they were boozers," Josie said. "They drank like fish."

"Well, that could be another way of saying it," Ethel said.

"Unfortunately," Ethel continued, "even having a son didn't keep them together. They argued and fought many times over the years, I was told, and eventually, Arthur grew fed up and told Joanne to leave."

"When did she leave?" Michelle asked.

"I'm trying to recall," Ethel said. "I believe it was the same year he died. Earlier of course."

"Nineteen sixty-three," Michelle said.

"Why yes, child, how did you know?"

"We found some stories in the newspaper from back then," Corey said, "About Mr. Cooper being killed and then about his funeral."

Ethel closed her eyes for a moment.

"So sad," she said. "Robert and I came over for the funeral and tried to comfort his mother."

"That was December, right?" Michelle asked.

"Yes, I believe it was," Ethel said. "Arthur died around Thanksgiving, if I remember correctly."

"That's what we read in the paper," Corey said.

"Ma'am," Michelle asked, "do you remember anything about their son Phillip?"

"Now let me think," Ethel said. "I do remember people saying how tragic it was for the Coopers with Arthur dying after his wife had run off and now his son was missing too. Everyone thought it was just a shame."

"Do you remember anything about his disappearance?" Corey asked.

"I seem to recall they said he just never came home one day," Ethel said. "A Wednesday, if I remember right."

"But his father didn't do anything," Michelle said, "at least not for a few days."

"Those were different times, my dear," Ethel said. "Men worked long hours and women were expected to take care of the children. Not like today when everyone appears to be all tied together.

"And I do remember being told Arthur did report it to the police."

"But no one looked for him later," Michelle said. "Why not?"

"Oh, I don't know," Ethel replied. "I suppose no one thought to since the family was gone."

"Didn't anyone try to contact Mrs. Cooper?" Corey asked.

"No one knew where she was," Ethel said. "When Arthur threw her out, she left Wagner County and went who knows where. We never heard from her again."

"Maybe folks thought Phil ran off to be with his mother," Josie said.

"That's very possible, Josephine," Ethel said. "That's very possible."

"Everyone just forgot about him, didn't they?" Michelle said.

"Perhaps," Ethel said.

No one spoke for several seconds.

"That's a heck of a story, Aunt Ethel," Josie said finally. "I didn't know any of that."

"It's good to learn new things," Ethel said. "And I hope you two young people learned something. I hope you heard what you needed."

"We certainly learned a lot," Corey said.

"But we're sorry if we brought up bad memories," Michelle said. "We didn't mean to make you sad."

"You haven't, my dear," Ethel replied. "If anything, you've made me curious."

"What do you mean, Aunt Ethel?" Josie asked.

"Well, if the body these children discovered really is our missing young Phillip, I certainly would like to know," Ethel said. "Our family needs closure."

"Would you like us to let you know what else we find out?" Michelle asked.

"Oh, most certainly."

Miss Ethel placed her glass on the end table and stood.

"I am so glad you came," she said. "It is wonderful to meet new people, especially young ones."

Michelle closed her notebook and she and Corey stood up. They offered their hands to Miss Ethel and the old woman shook each.

"Thank you so much," she said. "Do come and visit again. Even if it isn't to finish the story."

"Thank you, ma'am," the kids replied.

"Josephine," Ethel said, turning to her great-niece, "Are you still driving that beautiful old car?"

"Oh yes!" Josie said, "It is great."

"Indeed it is," Ethel said. "Now I know you can't today, as I'm sure you must see your young friends home, but you must bring it when you come again.

"You can take me for a drive."

Josie smiled and nodded.

Lela showed them to the front door, saying nothing until they were on the porch.

"Behave yourself, Josephine," she said. "You must do that for your aunt's sake."

"Yes, Lela," Josie said.

She walked quickly to the car, ahead of Corey and Michelle.

Josie took off her sandals and tossed them into the car. Then she reached in and grabbed a bag from behind the front seat.

"Close your eyes," she said, whipping her dress over her head and tossing it into the car.

Seeing her naked, save for her panties, Michelle blushed and turned away.

Corey just stared at the young woman with his jaw hanging open.

Josie pulled a tank top from the bag and slipped it on. As she pulled the tight shirt over her chest, she saw Corey gaping at her.

"I told you to close your eyes," Josie said evenly. She took a pair of short denim cut-offs from the bag and pulled them on.

"Okay, let's go," she said. Michelle turned around and walked toward the driver's door. Corey didn't move.

"Hey!" Josie said sharply to Corey. "I said let's go! Get in the car, dude."

Corey shook his head and went around to the passenger side.

As Josie moved the seat-back so Michelle could climb in, she leaned into the younger girl and spoke quietly.

"Girl, you best watch yourself."

"What do you mean?" Michelle asked.

"I think I just kick-started that boy's juices," Josie replied.

"Huh?"

"Ask your mama about it," Josie said, putting the seat back to its original position.

"Better yet, never mind. You'll figure it out soon enough."

Before closing her door and starting the car, Josie slipped on her Chuck Taylors.

"Did you kids get what you needed?" Josie asked, as she turned the key.

"I think so," Michelle said. "I took a lot of notes."

Corey didn't answer. They were down the hill and a couple miles back toward town before his head cleared.

"Uh, can I ask something?" he said.

"That depends, kid," Josie said. "What about?"

"Does Miss Ethel really like this car?"

"Sure," Josie said, "why not? It was hers to begin with. Well, hers and Uncle Robert's. But I never met him. He died before I was born."

"How'd you end up driving it?"

"My daddy bought it when Aunt Ethel couldn't drive anymore. Lela couldn't stand it, so we took it."

"But Aunt Ethel still likes to ride in it?" Michelle asked.

"You know it," Josie said. "It's the one part of visiting her I like doing. It's why I brought the change of clothes, in case she wanted to go for a drive.

"Aunt Ethel just loves getting out on the country roads with the top down and the wind blowing through. She says it helps keep her alive."

The kids gave Josie directions to each of their houses and she dropped them off in turn. Both were ready to take it easy the rest of the day, though they were looking forward to their meeting at the *Record / Times* the next morning

XII

When they entered Judge Danielson's office the next morning, he was placing some papers on Annette's desk before heading to the weekly conference. As the judge told Mrs. Palmer what the papers were about, Corey and Michelle grabbed their pens and notepads before heading over to the newspaper office.

Before the judge or the kids could leave, Chief Judge Barker came into the office.

"Good morning, all," he said. "I'm glad everyone's here."

"What's going on, Your Honor?" Judge Danielson asked.

"Well, Theo," Barker said. "I'm a little concerned about what's been happening here in your chambers."

"I don't understand, sir."

"It would appear, Judge Danielson, your two young investigators have stirred up a bit of ruckus."

"Oh dear," Annette said.

"Indeed," Barker said. "I got a call from Rich Geltsin over at the *Record / Times* on Saturday. Something about a file he wanted to look at, but couldn't get Chief Blaise or Sheriff Wingate to release it."

No one said anything.

"Now I didn't have the slightest idea what he was talking about." Judge Barker continued, "But then Mr. Geltsin told me you suggested he call me if he had problems getting it."

"Yes, sir, I did," Danielson said.

"That's what I figured." Barker said. "So I told our friend from the newspaper I'd take care of it."

"What did you do, sir?" Annette asked.

"I simply called both men and told them if one of them didn't release that file to Mr. Geltsin by Sunday night, I'd see both of them in my court this morning to explain why they wouldn't."

"And if I didn't like their reasons," the Chief Judge continued, "I'd hold both of them in contempt."

"Did they release the file?" Danielson asked.

"He had it before supper that night."

Annette and Judge Danielson laughed. Corey and Michelle didn't quite understand what the adults were talking about, so they stayed quiet.

"We should go, Judge," Barker said. "Shouldn't keep our colleagues waiting."

Barker turned to leave and saw the kids.

"And here are the troublemakers themselves," he said, "Still digging up leads?"

"Yessir," Corey stammered, "I guess."

"We didn't mean to make trouble," Michelle said.

"Oh good heavens, you two," Barker said chuckling. "You haven't. And even if you had, I'd tell you keep at it.

"This has been more interesting than most summers around here, hasn't it, Theo?"

"Yes, sir, it has," Danielson said.

"Are you off to the break room again?" Barker asked.

"No, sir," Corey said, "We're going over to the *Record / Times*."

"Mr. Geltsin says he has some information for us," Michelle said.

"Well, good luck to you," Barker said.

Corey and Michelle walked into the newspaper office just a few minutes after nine o'clock. The usual morning meeting was over, but the same two reporters who messed with them the last time were leaving together again.

"Hey, Chief," one said, "You're two CI's are here."

"If that's what they are," the other said. "Maybe they're unnamed sources."

"Are you sure you won't tell us what's up, Boss?" the first one said.

"I will not," Geltsin said firmly from back among the desks, "Get out of here, you two, and hit the streets. We've still got a paper to put out today."

The reporters once again left the office chuckling.

"Good to see you again," Geltsin said to the kids, motioning them back to his desk. "I've got something on that number you showed me."

Once seated, Geltsin showed the kids the number again, this time written larger on a full sheet of paper.

"Okay," he said, "this number of yours. You said you didn't recognize it or understand what it was."

"No, sir," Corey said.

"Have you ever seen any number like it?" Geltsin asked.

They looked at the number, but both kids shook their heads after a few seconds.

"Alright, let's try this," the editor said, taking the paper back. He wrote the letters *"J"* and *"L"* next to the number and gave the sheet back to the kids.

"How about this?"

Corey and Michelle looked at the new writing.

"It sort of looks like a phone number," Michelle said.

Geltsin smiled. "That's right. That's exactly what it is."

"But phone numbers are just that," Corey said. "Numbers. There aren't any letters in them."

"That's very true, young man," Geltsin said. "But that's today. It wasn't always that way."

He pulled a very old phone book out of the desk drawer. "Here's how things used to be," he said, opening the directory and turning it so Corey and Michelle could see the listings.

"Back in the fifties and sixties, phone numbers weren't the same way we have them now. In fact, people didn't always use numbers."

"How did they make a call?" Michelle asked.

"Originally, every city and town had their own little phone company and their own operators," Geltsin explained. "In small places like here, people picked up the phone and either cranked the handle or something to ring a bell and get the operator's attention. Then they'd say who they wanted to talk to and the operator would connect them."

"That sounds really slow," Corey said.

"It was," Geltsin continued, "and it took a lot of operators too, especially in the big cities."

"So the phone company invented direct dialing and people could call each other on their own. But that meant every phone needed a number."

He pointed to the book. "And that's where these came in. Each phone now had its own number."

Michelle looked closer at the faded white page of names and numbers.

"But all these only have five numbers," she said. "Phones have seven."

"That's true," Geltsin said, "But you didn't need to list all of them because the first two were the same for everyone."

He flipped to another part of the book, opening part of the old fashioned Yellow Pages.

"Back here, all the numbers have seven." He pointed to a business at random. "Well, seven characters. Every one begins with *J-L-5*.

"All the residential listings begin the same way, so they left off the *J-L*."

"Why *J-L*?" Corey asked.

"That was the name of the exchange," Geltsin said. "It stood for *Jewel*. That's where it was located, next to Jewel Creek over by the county line. Our phone system covered Wagner, Jameson, and Morris counties."

"You see, when the phone company set this up, they also connected all those individual systems so people could call other folks in other places." Geltsin continued. "Thing was, they needed a way to tell each area apart. So they named each place where the local lines came together and used two letters from that name as the first two characters in the phone number. Then they figured out if they used the next character as part of the exchange and not the actual number, they could have a lot more phones in an area.

"It worked great in places where there were lots of people and lots of phones, though we really didn't need it here."

"Why not?" Michelle asked.

"There weren't that many phones," Geltsin said. "Not like today where there are more phones than people, not to mention modems, cable lines, cell phones, and all that."

"But phones don't use letters anymore," Corey said.

"Really?" Geltsin said. "Have you checked your dialing display? The letters are still there."

"But you're right," he continued. "Using the letter prefixes stopped in the late sixties. By this time, the phone company connected everything into one huge network and people could call anyone anywhere directly. Of course, that's why we also have area codes and sometimes have to dial ten or eleven numbers to get someone. Using just the numbers was easier for their programming and system."

"Wow," Michelle said, "I never knew all this."

"I didn't either," Geltsin said. "I'm not that old and had to look most of it up."

Corey pointed to the page with their original number. "So you think this is an old phone number?"

"I sure do," Geltsin said.

"Can we trace it?" Corey asked.

"We can do something easier than that," Geltsin said. "We can call it." He punched the speaker option on his desk phone and dialed the number. He used the keypad to add the *J-L* to the other digits. The phone on the other end rang.

"Storm's Drug Store," a man answered. Corey and Michelle looked at each other.

"Morning, Bill," Geltsin said. "Rich Geltsin. How're things today?"

"Doing great, Rich," the drug store owner replied. "What can I help you with this morning?"

"You remember that thing I talked to you about last week? About folks looking into something from a long time ago?"

"Yes I do. "What about it?"

"Well, I've got the two lead investigators here with me now, and I wondered if we might come by and talk to you about it. Is that a problem?"

"I think that would be okay. But give me about twenty minutes to wrap some things up."

"See you then," Geltsin said and disconnected.

"How did you find whose number it was?" Michelle asked.

"I didn't have to," Geltsin said. "I recognized it as soon as I saw it. Storm's Drug Store has had that phone number for as long as I can remember. When I looked at your scrap of paper last week, I knew immediately who the number belonged to.

"I didn't want to say anything until I talked to Mr. Storm first. That's why I asked you over this morning. I wanted to tell you the history and then ask Bill if he'd talk to you."

He got up from the desk. "So let's get going."

"We need to let our moms know," Corey said, reaching for his own phone.

A few minutes later, they were outside, walking from the *Record / Times* to Storm's Drug Store on the square.

Betsy Clark worked the front counter as usual. Bill Storm only had five or six employees, and he was both the owner and the registered pharmacist. Another clerk switched off with Betsy, with one covering each weekend day, and two assistants helped with prescriptions. A full-time person took care of inventory and stocking shelves with a part-time helper who also made deliveries.

"He's up in the office," Betsy said as they walked in. Geltsin and the kids walked back toward the pharmacy area. They climbed the stairs next to it.

The second floor contained several rooms off the hallway. Bill Storm sat behind a large cluttered desk in the first room.

"Hey Rich," Storm said as the three entered.

"Hi, Bill," Geltsin said as they shook hands. "Thanks for letting me bring these two over. This is Corey and Michelle."

"Nice to meet you," Mr. Storm said, "and it's no problem. But what's this all about?"

"I better let them tell you," Geltsin said. "It's their story."

"Okay," Storm said, "have a seat, you two, and let's talk."

"Now Rich tells me you want to know about a phone number," he said as Corey and Michelle sat down.

"Yes, sir," Michelle said, "We found it in an old wallet."

"It was on a torn piece of paper," Corey said, "and only had five digits. But Mr. Geltsin said it could have been how somebody wrote a number down."

"He explained how phone calls and numbers used to work," Michelle said. "And then he called it and got the drugstore."

"That's not surprising," Storm replied. "That's been our phone number since…"

"Well, since forever," he continued. "At least the last four numbers have been the phone number here since my grandfather opened the place after the Second World War."

"Even the rest of the number hasn't changed much over the years, has it Bill?" Geltsin said.

"Nope," Storm replied. "Still the same, even with the changes in the prefix."

"Kids, it's like I told you," Geltsin said, "I recognized the number as soon as I saw it last week. But I wanted to check it out with Bill before I said anything to you. I wanted to make sure it was okay if you looked into it."

"And I'm happy to talk to you," Storm said, "but I don't think there's much I can tell."

Geltsin's phone buzzed.

"Hang on," he said, answering the call. He listened for a few seconds and said he'd be there as soon as he could.

"Sorry, guys," he said. "I have to go. Problem out at the plant."

"Are you two okay getting back wherever?" he asked Corey and Michelle.

They nodded and Geltsin left.

Afterward, Mr. Storm picked up the conversation.

"Okay, what's important about my phone number?"

"We don't know," Corey said. "We just found it on the body up in the clock tower."

"You're the two kids who found that thing?" Storm asked.

"Yes, sir," Michelle said.

They explained how'd they climbed up, gotten trapped, and found the body. They also told Mr. Storm about finding the library card and then their research and the newspaper stories and what the medical examiner's report said.

They finished with what they'd heard from Josie and Miss Ethel about the Coopers.

"That is one heckuva story, kids," Storm said when they'd finished, "but I don't see how I can add anything to it."

"I've never heard of Phillip Cooper," he continued, "and I wasn't even around back then."

"But he had your phone number," Corey said. "Why?"

"Like I said," Storm replied, "it's been the store's number since the beginning. Maybe he needed to remember it so he could talk to someone here."

"Who would he talk to?" Michelle asked.

"No clue," Storm said. "It was a long time ago. Nineteen sixty-three, right?"

"Yes, sir."

"And you said he was how old?"

"Dr. Driscoll said somewhere between twelve and fifteen."

Storm thought for a few seconds.

"You know, my dad was about that age then, maybe he'd know."

"Is your father still alive?" Michelle asked.

"Do you think we could talk to him?" Corey added.

"Yes and maybe," Storm replied, "Depends on what shape he's in."

"Where is he?" Corey asked.

"He's in the nursing home south of town," Storm said.

"Why?" Michelle asked. "Is he that old?"

"Good lord, no," Storm said. "But he was hurt pretty bad and needs a lot of help."

"You see, about ten years ago," he explained, "my folks had an explosion and fire at their house. Gas leak, they said, and my mother was killed."

"We're sorry," Michelle said.

"It's okay," Storm said. "It was an accident.

"Anyway, my dad was hurt when the ceiling collapsed on him and now he can't walk. He also inhaled a lot of smoke before they got him out, so he can't breathe real well, either, these days."

"But why doesn't he live with you?" Corey asked. "Couldn't you take care of him?"

"I could," Storm said, "but I spend all my time here, running the store.

"But that's okay, Dad understands. It was the same when he ran things; he spent most of his time here. So did my grandfather, but it was a little easier then. They lived up here above the place."

"Really?" Michelle said.

"Really," Storm replied. "That's the way it was back then. A lot of business owners lived above or behind their stores. Most of them didn't make enough money to buy a separate place.

"Heck, I might move back in here myself some day. Walking downstairs to work would sure beat driving several miles."

"So do you think your father would talk to us?" Corey asked.

"I can find out. I usually visit him several times a week, and if you don't mind the way the place smells, we can go out there today. That is, if he's up to it."

"We'd have to ask our moms," Corey said.

"Okay, you do that, and I'll see if my dad is up to some extra visitors."

They each made calls. Bill Storm had the easiest one. He could visit any time, and he only needed to find if his father, Fred, was feeling well enough. According to the nurse answering his call, the old man was doing fine that day.

Corey and Michelle had it tougher. Neither of their mothers had a problem with them going with Mr. Storm. Everyone in Craigsville knew the druggist and both women trusted him. The problem was whether the kids would disturb people at the home.

"We'll behave," both said.

"We just want to ask Mr. Storm's father about Phillip Cooper."

Annette and Marybelle finally said yes after each talked to Bill Storm directly. He promised to get them back by the time both women finished work for the day.

XIII

The drive to Magnolia Valley Nursing Home took about twenty-five minutes. On the way, Bill Storm told them about the place and about what to expect when meeting his father.

"Like most everything here, the place was a farm," he said. "But then a couple of doctors bought the place looking to get away from big city stress."

"Unfortunately, they found a little too much relaxation and couldn't run a farm for anything."

"So they changed it into a nursing home?" Michelle asked.

"Uh-huh," Storm said, "about thirty years ago."

"So we're just going to an old farmhouse?" Corey said.

"No, there's a lot more to it now," Storm said. "They've added new buildings and a small hospital, and I don't think they even use the old house anymore."

"Now don't try to wear my dad out," he added. "He gets tired easily."

"We won't," Michelle said, "but do you think he'll remember anything?"

"Heavens yes," Storm said. "Old Fred's mind still works perfectly."

"What should we call him?" Corey asked. "We can't call both of you Mr. Storm."

Bill Storm thought for a second. "Why don't you call him Mr. Fred. He'll get a kick out of it."

"Should we call you Mr. Bill? Corey asked.

"No," the druggist replied, smiling at the kids. They were much too young to know the name's old reference.

They parked in the visitors' lot and went in. Fred Storm wasn't in his room, but sat on the sun porch at the end of his floor. The room had several tables with chairs around them and some sofas along the walls. A large-screen TV hung from one corner where everyone could see it, but it was turned off at the moment.

It reminded the kids a little of Ethel Cooper's sun room, but without the fancier furniture.

Fred Storm sat in a wheelchair at one table with three regular chairs. He wore a lightweight long-sleeved shirt and light trousers. An oxygen tank was strapped on the back of his chair and a thin breathing tube went around his head into his nostrils.

"How're you doing today, Pop?" Bill Storm asked as he and the kids walked up.

"Hanging in there," the old man rasped. "Doing what I can."

"They still treating you alright?" Bill asked.

"Yep," Fred said. "Even take me outside these days, letting me enjoy the weather."

"Good to hear it," Bill told his father. "I guess I better tell you why I brought these two young ones out here to see you.

"They've got a very interesting story, Pop, and somehow our phone number's a part of it."

"Well, let's start with who you are," Fred Storm said. "Don't think I know you."

"Corey Palmer."

"Michelle Pritchard."

Fred looked at Michelle.

"Pete Pritchard's old pick up," he said, "I can see why he chose like he did. Don't you think so, Billy?"

"Come to think of it Pop, I do," Bill said. "Hadn't made the connection."

"What are you talking about?" Michelle asked.

"Honey," Fred said, "I know you're too young to remember, but your dad used to have a beautifully restored nineteen fifty-five dark blue Chevrolet pick-up truck. Did he ever tell you about it?"

"I've seen pictures of an old truck," Michelle said.

"Thing ran even better than it looked," Fred continued, "but he ended up selling it. Said he had to choose."

"Choose between what?" Corey asked.

"Pete told us he couldn't afford both the Chevy and the Shelly," Fred said. "He figured you'd turn out a lot cuter, and bring him more joy.

"I bet he was right, too."

As Corey and Bill laughed, Michelle blushed and lowered her head.

"I hadn't heard that story," Corey said. "It's great."

Michelle looked at Corey. "You better not tell *anyone*, Corey, I mean it!"

"Okay, you two," Bill said, "let's get to why you're here."

"Well, Mr. Fred," Corey said, "We wanted to ask you why somebody would've had your phone number in their wallet."

"Why not?" Fred said. "People need to call the drug store."

"Yes, sir," Michelle said, "But this was over fifty years ago."

"What?" Fred exclaimed. "Fifty years ago! Maybe you better tell me the story."

Corey and Michelle told Fred how they climbed into the tower, got stuck, and found the body up by the bell works."

"We found a wallet on the body with your phone number written on a scrap of paper," Corey said.

"We also found some old money and a library card with his name," Michelle said. "At least we think it's his name."

"What's the name?" Fred asked.

"Phillip Cooper."

Fred Storm froze. Tears began falling slowly from each eye and he bent over the table.

"No, god no." He began muttering, "No Phil, *no*. That wasn't supposed to happen."

"It can't be you."

He began shaking and sobbing heavily. Soon his heaves became gasps for breath. He tried to draw air into his lungs, but the damaged organs wouldn't take in enough to counter the sobs wracking his whole body.

"Dad, what's wrong?" Bill asked, moving to his father. "Dad, are you alright!?"

"Somebody go get help!"

Corey got up and ran from the room. "Hey!" he called as he moved down the hallway, "Somebody help!"

A nurse came running the opposite way. He ran past Corey to the sun porch. Seeing Fred Storm's struggles, the nurse punched the intercom button just inside the doorway.

"I need a cart to B-Wing sun porch, *STAT.*"

The nurse then went to Fred. He quickly removed the nostril tubes, changed something on the oxygen tank strapped to the back and placed a full-sized mask over Fred's nose and mouth.

"Breathe, Fred," he said, "come on. Slow breaths in and out. You can do this."

The heaving subsided, and Fred began taking deeper and more regular breaths.

"What happened?" the nurse asked.

"He got some distressing news," Bill Storm said. "Is he going to be alright?"

"I think so. I'll cancel the cart," the nurse said. "But you have to be more careful. His lungs can't really take this."

"We'll be careful," Bill said.

The nurse reattached Fred's nostril tubes, but he left the full mask available in case of another attack.

After the nurse left, Bill spoke to the kids.

"I guess we better leave, let my dad rest."

Fred raised his head.

"No, don't go," he said. "I need to say this. I've been holding onto this for too long, and I'm tired. It's time someone heard it."

Corey, Michelle, and Bill Storm sat down again.

Fred took some more seconds to compose himself and get his breathing back to sort of normal. With only twenty percent lung capacity, this was not an easy task.

"I've never told this to anyone," he said, "Didn't think I ever would. But I know that's my friend, Phil Cooper, you found, because I know how he got up there."

"What happened?" Corey asked, taking out his pad and pen to make notes.

"Like I said, Phil and I were friends. We were in the same classes all the way until we got to high school that year, and we still had some classes together.

"We used to mess around together after school. Sometimes we'd come down to the drug store and hang around until one of his folks or someone came to pick him up.

"Phil was always trying to find ways to skate close to trouble. I guess he figured his family would keep him out of any real problems."

Fred took several deep breaths from the tank.

"And one thing he wanted to do was climb up into the clock tower. I'll never forget that day…"

"Come on, Freddy," Phil said. "Haven't you wondered how far you can see from up there?"

"Not really," Fred replied. "Besides, we'll get caught."

"Not if we sneak in right when the place closes. They won't know."

"But people are still around, and how will we get out afterwards? The place will be all locked up."

"Okay, here's what we'll do. After we find where to get into the tower, I'll climb up and you come back down and keep lookout. I'll holler down to prove I made it and then come let you in."

"Then it's your turn."

"That's what we did," Fred recalled. "We found the access up on the third floor and then I went back outside. I kind of wandered around, trying not to get noticed, and about five minutes later, Phil hollered down…"

"Hey, Fred! Look at me. I made it." There was enough light for Fred to see him in the vent window above the clock face.

"Okay, great man. Now come on down."

A couple of minutes later, Phil hollered down again.

"Fred, I'm stuck. I can't get the trap door opened. Come help."

"I went to the big front doors, but they were locked. I started around the building trying to find a door or window still open, but couldn't find any."

"When I got around to the back of the building, across from city hall and the police station, I started trying to force a window open. That's when the cop got me…"

"What are you up to boy?" the officer said. "You trying to break in here? Trying to get in and cause mischief?"

"No, sir," Fred answered. *"I need to get in there because—"*

"You got no reason, boy, and I don't know what you're up to, but I can run you in. What's your name?"

"Fred Storm and I've got to—"

"You've got to nothin', boy," the officer said, *"And your daddy's not gonna be very happy about this. His son out trying to break into a building. Let's go."*

"He marched me over to the drugstore and told my father where he'd caught me. When my dad opened the door, I knew I was in for it. He was already drinking after closing up the store.

"I tried to explain, but Dad just smacked my face and told me to shut up. Then he told the officer he'd handle it."

"That's not right," Michelle said.

"I know," Fred replied, "but that's how things were. And it got worse. After the officer left, Dad started pulling off his belt to whip me..."

"Dad, honest," Fred cried. "It's not what you think. I need to help—"

"How dare you, boy," Sam Storm said. "Bringing dishonor on me by having the police catch you doing Lord only knows what. You're going to pay for this, stupid, and starting right now!"

"I ran through the store and made it up to my room." Fred paused to take several breaths.

"I'm sorry, Pop," Bill Storm said, "I never knew any of this."

"It's why I never laid a hand on you, son," Fred said. "I may have yelled at you and grounded you for stuff, but I never wanted to be like my old man."

"So what happened?" Corey asked. "Didn't you tell somebody later?"

"Well, young man," Fred replied, "though I made it to my room, my dad locked me in there until Friday. I guess he called the school to say I'd be out for a couple of days, and I was stuck there.

"Mama finally brought me some food and let me out, but she didn't want to hear a thing about what happened."

231

"And I guess I was too scared," Fred continued. "I didn't want to anger my old man again. And with everything else happening over the next few days, I don't think I could have gotten anybody to listen to me."

"You mean Phil's father, Mr. Cooper being killed?" Michelle asked.

"There was that, too," Fred said.

"Didn't you ever wonder if Phil ever got out?" Corey asked.

"I always figured he found a way or got somebody's attention," Fred answered.

"Even though you never saw him again?" Michelle said.

"Well, honey, I guessed he'd gotten out and then run off after his father was killed. His mama was gone by then too, so he didn't have any real family left."

"But now you're saying he never got out." Fred lowered his head and started sobbing. No great heaves this time, but steady tears and some shaking.

"I'm so sorry," he said quietly. "I didn't mean to." He started crying harder.

"Take it easy, Pop," Bill said, "Don't hurt yourself."

"I killed my friend. I left him trapped up there."

Corey and Michelle looked at each other. They hadn't brought their notes and files, but remembered what was in them."

"Mr. Fred," Michelle said, "I don't think you did."

Fred looked up, still crying.

"According to Dr. Driscoll's report, Phillip Cooper died because he fell and hit his head," Corey said. "And he also got his hand caught in the gears, which ripped apart his wrist."

"But I left him trapped up there," Fred said.

"You tried to get him out," Michelle said. "You wanted to tell someone."

"But I failed," Fred replied.

The others were silent.

"I think we should go," Bill Storm said. "You get some rest, Pop. I'll come back later."

Corey and Michelle gathered their things and started to leave. Fred Storm just sat in his chair.

No one spoke on the drive back to the square. When they reached the drug store, Michelle spoke as the all got out.

"We're really sorry, Mr. Storm," she said. "We didn't mean to upset your father."

Bill Storm sighed. "I'm sorry too. I didn't know any of that. The old guy held the secret for a long time."

"So what's going to happen?" Corey asked. "Now that somebody knows."

"I guess that's up to you," Storm said. "Are you going to tell anyone?"

The kids looked at each other. "We don't have to," Michelle said. "We're just doing this because we found the body and wanted to know."

"Yeah, but Mr. Geltsin asked us to tell him what we found out," Corey said.

"Can you hold off on that?" Bill asked. "A least for a time while I figure out what to do about my dad."

The kids nodded and began walking back to the courthouse.

XIV

Corey and Michelle were back in Judge Danielson's office the next morning. Seeing them start gathering their things, the judge asked where they were off to.

"The break room, I guess," Corey said. "We're going to start organizing everything and see what we've learned."

"It's like everyone's told us," Michelle said, "We need to figure out what it all means."

"Good for you," Danielson said. "I'm looking forward to hearing the story."

"Yes, sir," Corey said. "But our problem is we've got so much stuff, we almost don't have enough space on the tables downstairs."

Michelle nodded.

"Well, then," Danielson said, "Why don't you go down to the conference room? There's plenty of space and I don't think anything's scheduled for today."

Annette checked her computer and confirmed the room's availability.

Corey and Michelle smiled and each grabbed a box and headed to the conference room.

"You two behave down there," Annette said as they left.

With Dr. Driscoll's report, the state crime lab findings, their newspaper copies, and all the notes taken from meetings with the Storms, Miss Ethel, and others, they had a lot of materials.

They also had two sets of everything, one set in each box so they could look at things separately or together. Michelle began spreading her papers and copies out on the large table. She left the autopsy and forensic file for last.

"What are you doing?" Corey asked.

"Putting things in order," Michelle said, "So we can figure out what we've got and what we're missing."

Corey followed along, but left much of his information boxed. He did add the copies of the dollars and the birth certificate to their layout. He held his notes on Fred Storm's story for last.

"Okay, now what?" he asked when they finished.

"Now let's write it all down," Michelle said, "And come up with what it means."

"You mean like a report?" Corey said.

"Sort of."

"Jeez, Shel," Corey whined, "We're not doing homework here. This isn't school."

"Oh come on, Corey," Michelle said. "How else are we going to figure out all this stuff? We need to write it down."

"Besides," she continued, "if we have to do a Social Studies project next year, we'll already have this."

"Okay," Corey said, "so where do we start?"

Michelle took a notepad out of her box. She opened it to a fresh page and grabbed her pen. She started with a title for the write-up.

"I'm going to call it *The Body in the Tower,* okay?"

Corey shrugged.

"Let's start with a time-line," Michelle said. "Tell me the dates when everything happened and then we'll fill in the details and all the other things we've found."

Corey moved to the first set of papers on the table.

"Okay," he said. "Phillip Cooper was born on March nineteenth, nineteen forty-nine. His parents were Arthur and Joanne Cooper."

"Got it," Michelle said. "What's next?"

"Well," Corey said, "the next date we have is nineteen fifty-seven from the dollar bill in his wallet."

"That's not part of the time-line," Michelle said.

"It's a date," Corey said. Michelle shook her head and wrote it down.

"Okay, next is the library card. That was issued in nineteen sixty-one."

"Okay, then what?" Michelle said.

"Then we've got the date on the other bill," Corey said, "nineteen sixty-three. This proves he didn't disappear until late in the year."

"Corey," Michelle said, "we already *know* when he disappeared. The date's in the paper."

"Okay, okay," he said, moving to the newspaper copies. "Here are the dates from the articles.

Corey read off all the dates. When Phillip Cooper was last seen, when his father reported it to the police, the date of the story itself, and then the dates Arthur Cooper died and his funeral.

"That's it, I guess," he said, "until we found him up there last month."

Michelle wrote that date down too.

"I guess now we need to write down why we think the body we found really is Phillip Cooper," she said.

"You mean besides what Mr. Fred told us?" Corey asked. Michelle nodded.

Corey went to the last and largest set of papers, the file from the medical examiner and the state crime lab.

"The autopsy report and the other lab reports say the body was up in the tower for fifty years or so, and the person was twelve to fifteen years old. That fits."

"And we did find the library card on him," Michelle added.

Corey looked through the lab reports again. "I thought I saw something about DNA tests."

He found the right page. "Here it is." He read silently for a few seconds.

"What does it say?" Michelle asked.

"Rats," Corey said. "It says they did pull enough from the body to run tests, but all that's here is a profile. No identification since there wasn't anything to compare it to."

"So I guess we can't really prove it's Phillip Cooper, can we?" Michelle said. "Unless we use Mr. Fred's story."

"I guess not," Corey said, "But I'm pretty sure, aren't you?"

"Uh-huh," Michelle said. "With all this and what Miss Ethel told us about the parents, I'm pretty sure too."

"And we know how he got trapped up there," Corey said, "because we got trapped the same way."

"But we don't know what happened in between," he continued. "We don't know why nobody ever climbed up there and found him a long time ago."

"Who would know that?" Michelle asked.

"I don't know," Corey said. "Maybe some of the older people around here."

"Maybe Mr. Hingstrom, the building guy, would know," Michelle said.

"You're right," Corey said. "Let's go ask him."

"You go ahead," Michelle said, taking out her other notebook, "I'm going to put what Miss Ethel and Josie told us into the time-line."

"Take notes," she added as he left the conference room.

Corey didn't know where to find the building supervisor, but thought the man would most likely be in the basement.

He didn't find Mr. Hingstrom in any open room, but found two members of Judge Rollins's staff in the break room.

"Hey kid," one staffer said, "nice of you to let us have our break area back."

Corey didn't react to the comment. "Have you seen Mr. Hingstrom?" he asked.

"Not recently," the other staffer said, "but you might check his office."

"Where's that?" Corey asked.

"Down this hall and make a left around the corner. Next to the furnace room."

Corey walked to the end of the corridor and turned left. He didn't need more direction as he heard noise from an open door. He looked into the furnace room itself and saw Hingstrom working at an open panel on one of the large units.

Summer was perfect for doing routine maintenance and upgrades to the courthouse heating system. The air conditioning system was independent and its machinery was on the opposite side of the building. These furnaces wouldn't be needed for two or three more months, so Mr. Hingstrom could take the time and keep them in proper shape.

He did the same with the air conditioning system in January each year.

"Mr. Hingstrom?" Corey called.

"Yeah, what do you need?" Hingstrom replied without looking up.

"If you've got a few minutes," Corey said, "I'd like to ask you about the clock in the tower.

Hingstrom looked up at Corey. "Don't tell me you want to climb back up there."

"No, sir," Corey said, "I just want to ask you about how it works and stuff."

"Alright," Hingstrom said, "I need a few more minutes here. Go wait in my office. It's just down this hallway on the other side.

Corey waited five minutes before Mr. Hingstrom came in. He hadn't touched anything as he didn't know what most of the stuff was. There were binders and papers on shelves, boxes on the floor, and tools everywhere. Hingstrom's desk could hardly be seen with all its clutter.

"Alright son, what can I help you with?" Hingstrom said, sitting down behind his desk.

"My friend Michelle and I are trying to find out about the body we found up in the tower," Corey said. "We think we know who he was and how he got trapped, but we're trying to figure out why he was up there so long.

"Why didn't anybody ever look up there?"

"Kind of wondered about that myself," Hingstrom replied. "I'd never been up there until we found you two."

"Why not? Don't you have to keep it working?"

"Nope. And that's probably why that poor kid wasn't found."

"Why don't you ever have to go up there?"

"Because there's nothing to do," the building supervisor said, "Everything we need to work on is down below or outside.

"Do you remember those two doors off the landing where you climb the ladder?"

Corey nodded.

"Well, behind one of them are tanks of oil and lubricants, along with pumps and pipes leading up into the works. That's how we keep everything running smoothly.

"Behind the other door are the motors, timers, and cables that control everything. It's how we keep all four clocks running together."

"But what about the clock faces, the hands and things?" Corey asked.

"Those are all on the outside," Hingstrom said, "so we climb up the side of the tower if needed to work on them."

"What about the bell?" Corey asked. "Where is it controlled from?"

"Same place. There's even a special timer to keep it from ringing at night. People didn't like having to hear it when they were trying to sleep."

"But the bell doesn't always ring on time. Why didn't anyone ever climb up to find out why?"

"Now that I really don't know," Hingstrom said. "I guess nobody ever cared."

Corey wrote this down along with everything else he'd heard.

"You know, maybe I should tell you the whole story of the clock," Hingstrom continued. "It might make things clearer."

"Do you know how old the courthouse is?"

"Over a hundred years, I think"

"That's right. And it was built to replace an older one the county simply outgrew. And there's always been a clock in the tower."

"Thing is," Hingstrom continued, "the one up there now isn't all that old. They put it in just around sixty years ago."

"What happened to the old one?" Corey asked.

"Well, son," Mr. Hingstrom continued, "here's what I was told. Back during World War II, the country needed metal for planes, guns, bombs and things, so the county took all the old clockworks and bells out to donate for the war. The tower was empty for several years.

"Sometime during the fifties, people decided to replace the clock with a new modern one. So everybody chipped in. The city, the county, even the Cooper family gave a bunch of money, and a new clock and new bell were put up there."

"Was it always like it is today?" Corey asked.

"Sure was," Hingstrom said. "They installed the most modern and automatic clock works they could come up with. Wagner County wanted to show off how easy and smooth something even that big could run."

"Worked really well, too," he continued, "Nobody ever has to go up there unless something goes really wrong. And nothing ever has, at least as far as I know."

"But the bell's always off," Corey said.

"I know," Hingstrom said, "but that didn't start until later, and it's only gotten really bad in the last few years. I guess nobody ever thought about it.

"And it sort of made things fun, too. People began thinking we had our own time schedule."

Corey made more notes.

"Anything else?" Hingstrom asked.

"No, sir," Corey said, "except to ask if you sealed off the clock like the judge said."

"Hingstrom smiled. "Well, sort of. I fixed the latch on the trap door so it could be opened from both sides. Probably should have done it years ago. That way, you two never would've gotten stuck up there."

"Of course, then again," Hingstrom continued, "if you'd gotten out of there on your own, that body might still be up there."

While Corey talked to Mr. Hingstrom, Mrs. Palmer went to the conference room with lunch for the kids. Michelle looked up from her writing as Annette walked in.

"Where's Corey?" Annette asked.

"In the basement, I think," Michelle answered. "He went to ask Mr. Hingstrom something about the clock."

"What are you working on?" Annette asked.

"I'm writing down everything we've found out and trying to organize it."

Michelle put her pen down and massaged her right hand.

"What's wrong?" Annette asked.

"I'm not used to writing all this," Michelle said, "I usually use my computer."

Since Annette knew no computer was part of their grounding, she just nodded.

"Text Corey and tell him lunch is here," she said, turning around to leave.

Corey got Michelle's text as Mr. Hingstrom finished the story. He thanked the man for his time and went back upstairs.

As they ate lunch, Corey told Michelle what he'd learned.

"Mr. Hingstrom told me the clock runs on its own, so no one ever had to climb up there."

"And that's why the body was still there when we climbed up?" Michelle asked.

"I guess so."

"Okay, I'll write that down."

"What do we do next?" Corey asked.

"I want to get all this cleaned up," Michelle said, pointing to her pages of writing. "Then I don't know. It's not like we have to turn it in for a grade, or anything."

"I guess I should clean up my notes from the nursing home," Corey said.

"Do we really want to include that?"

"It really proves what happened."

"Yeah," Michelle said, "but I don't want to hurt Mr. Fred. I don't want him to go to jail or anything."

"Me neither," Corey said. "But Mr. Geltsin at the paper wanted to see what we found."

"I know, but I don't want to include that part."

"Okay. But let's take him the rest of it."

After finishing their sandwiches, Corey worked on re-writing his notes. He had to stop and massage his hand as well. When he finished, he began putting everything back in the boxes. He kept all the copies and files in order, in case they needed to pull something out later.

Michelle finished writing and gathered her notes.

As they we starting to leave, Corey spoke. "You know what, Shel? I just realized something else."

"What?"

"We're done with this," Corey said. "We've found probably everything we can."

"I know," Michelle said, "what about it?"

"What are we going to do next?" Corey said. "We're still grounded, so what can we do for the rest of the summer?"

Michelle didn't answer. They walked back to Judge Danielson's office in silence.

They set the boxes in the usual spot, next to the sofa in the outer office. Mrs. Palmer looked up when they came in.

"All finished?" she asked.

"Uh-huh," Corey said, "except for putting it all down."

"I'm going to do that if I can find a computer to use," Michelle said. "It's too hard to write it by hand."

"Something none of us like to do," Judge Danielson said as he walked out of his office.

"So what did you finally conclude?" he asked. "Was it Phillip Cooper?"

"We think so," Corey said. "Everything sure looks like it."

"And all of our information fits," Michelle added.

"That's great," Danielson said. "When can you tell us the whole story?"

The kids looked at each other. "Right now, if you want," Corey said.

Danielson chuckled. "Sorry, but right now won't work. I'm due at a meeting over in Jameson County this afternoon, and we've got all the usual paperwork and things to catch up on."

"But how about this?" he continued. "I do want to hear the story, and I'm pretty sure Judge Barker would too. And there's Mr. Geltsin over at the *Record / Times,* and I'd bet your mothers would like to know what's kept you so busy recently.

"Wouldn't you, Annette?"

Mrs. Palmer smiled. "Yes, I would."

"Okay," the judge said, "we'll do this. We don't have any trials or hearings scheduled after tomorrow morning, so let's have lunch in the conference room. We'll invite Judge Barker and the editor, and you two can present your findings."

"You mean like a report?" Michelle said.

"Well, not that formal," Danielson said.

"Can I invite my mom too?" Michelle asked.

"Certainly," the judge answered. "The more the merrier."

"We'll probably need copies of things for everyone," Corey said.

"And you can do that this afternoon and tomorrow morning," Annette replied. "I'll make the calls."

Corey and Michelle carefully made several copies of everything except their meeting write-ups and the forensic file. Everyone involved already had copies of that report.

She would try to get her mother to let her use her laptop that night to redo the notes.

Marybelle was happy to let her daughter use the computer for a real project, and it only took Michelle about an hour to type everything. She printed two copies, one for herself and one for Corey.

Her mom also agreed to come for lunch and the story.

Corey talked Annette into letting him use his computer that night too, and he easily typed in Fred Storm's story along with the history of the phone number. He printed two copies as well, but didn't show them to his mother.

XV

The next morning, Annette insisted Corey dress nicely. At least wear a school shirt, she told him.

"Aw, Mom," Corey said.

"Aw nothing, Corey," Annette replied. "These are important people you're talking to today, and you need to look your best."

"Besides, I'm sure Michelle will be dressed nicely, too."

She was. Marybelle told her to wear school clothes, so both kids were in oxford-cloth shirts and khaki slacks.

They spent the morning organizing things, making sets of papers for everyone. It didn't take long, so they also killed time quietly, trying not to disturb anyone.

"How do we do this?" Corey asked. "Do you want to tell the story, or me?"

"Why don't we take turns?" Michelle said. "Each of us can tell part of the story and then the other."

"Do we mention Mr. Fred and the phone number?"

"Not if we don't have to."

"Okay, you want to go first?"

"No way," Michelle said. "We have to start with finding the body, and that's all yours."

"Thanks a lot," Corey said. Michelle smiled.

There were sandwiches, potato salad, green salad, and drinks set up in the conference room. As everyone entered, they filled their plates and sat at the long table eating. Mr. Geltsin and Mrs. Pritchard arrived just after twelve noon and quickly filled plates to join the others.

"Alright, everyone," Judge Danielson said as the others finished lunch, "We're here to hear a story. Kids, the floor is yours."

Corey and Michelle stood and picked up the sets of pages to pass around. When they finished, they stood at the end of the room, by the seat Judge Barker normally filled during the weekly judicial conferences.

"Okay," Corey began, "I think everybody knows Michelle and I climbed up into the clock tower and found a body. It was really old and it was up there for a long time."

"We also found a library card in a wallet with the name, Phillip E. Cooper, along with two one-dollar bills. We made copies for everyone."

"Wait a second," Judge Barker said. "There wasn't anything in Dr. Driscoll's report about dollar bills."

"Uh, yessir, I know," Corey said sheepishly. "I stuffed them in my pocket and didn't find them until later."

"You know, some people might see that as withholding evidence," Judge Barker said, smiling.

"Oh, come on, judge," Geltsin said, "they documented everything and probably found out more than anyone over in the police or sheriff's offices would have."

"Alright, alright," Barker replied, chuckling. "Let's carry on."

The adults flipped pages and looked at card and the money as Corey picked up the story.

"Mr. Geltsin looked up the money and told us the newer one wasn't used until late in nineteen sixty-three," he said. "That meant the guy couldn't have been trapped up there before then."

"The library card was an adult one," Michelle said, "and I found his application for it over there. It was never renewed, so we think he died before it would have expired."

"But this gave you his name?" Judge Danielson asked.

"Uh-huh," Corey said, "and we found a birth certificate from nineteen forty-nine for Phillip Cooper. It also said who his parents were."

"The coroner's report said he was between twelve and fifteen," Michelle said, "so everything matches so far."

"Then Mr. Geltsin let us look through the old newspapers." Corey said. "We found a story on Phillip Cooper disappearing and the police were looking for information on him."

"The story said Phillip was last seen on Wednesday, November twentieth, nineteen sixty-three."

"It was from Friday's paper," Michelle said, "and also said his father had reported him missing the day before, Thursday."

"But then his father was killed that weekend." Corey said. "There was another article from the next week."

"And then one in early December about his funeral," Michelle added.

"That all fits," Judge Barker commented.

"So then we talked to Miss Ethel Cooper to ask about Phillip's parents," Corey said.

"She told us they were separated," Michelle said, "and that his mom was gone off somewhere. So then when Mr. Cooper was killed, nobody looked for Phillip anymore. She said everyone must have thought Phillip ran away to be with his mother."

"And nobody ever thought to look up in the clock tower," Corey said, "until we climbed up there last month."

"And that's what we didn't understand," Michelle said, finishing the story. "Why didn't anyone find him for so many years? Why didn't anybody keep looking?"

"You're right about that," Mr. Geltsin said. "You'd think someone would have gone up into the tower, even if it was just routine."

"Mr. Hingstrom told us the clock and bell run completely on their own," Corey said. "All he has to do is work in the rooms below, off the landing."

"So we guess there was no reason to check the clock tower and so no one found the body until we did," Michelle said. "But we really believe it's Phillip Cooper."

Corey nodded.

"And that's it?" Judge Danielson asked.

"Yes, sir," Corey said.

"Nothing came from that phone number you showed me?" Geltsin asked. "The one for Storm's Drugs?"

"Hold it," Judge Danielson said. "What phone number?"

"We also found a piece of paper in the wallet," Corey said. "There were numbers that turned out to be for Mr. Storm's drugstore. It was with the bills."

"So there's more evidence you withheld?" Judge Danielson said, smiling at Judge Barker. The chief judge smiled back.

"Remind me to have the chief or the sheriff teach these two about proper evidence," Barker said. Judge Danielson laughed.

"What about the nursing home?" Annette asked. "Did you learn anything from your visit there?"

"Hold on a second here," Geltsin said, "what nursing home visit?"

Corey and Michelle said nothing. They looked at each other and then down at their notes.

"Is there something more here, kids?" Judge Barker asked. "Something you don't want to tell us."

"Sort of," Corey mumbled.

"We kind of heard what really happened," Michelle added quietly, "but we don't want to get anyone in trouble."

"How would that happen?" Judge Danielson asked.

"Well, if somebody knew something and didn't say anything for a really long time," Corey said, "they might be in trouble because something bad happened."

"That's all true, young man," Judge Barker said, "but I think you ought to tell us what you learned and then we can figure out what should be done."

"It is kind of what we do around here," he continued, smiling.

"Spill it you two," Geltsin said. "Good investigative reporters always keep their editor in the loop.

"So let's have it."

Corey took a deep breath and began the story. "We told you about the piece of paper in the wallet with some numbers on it. We showed it to Mr. Geltsin who said he recognized it immediately. It's the number for the drug store."

"Mr. Geltsin explained how phone numbers changed over the years," Michelle said. "But Storm's Drug Store always used the same one for as long as he remembered."

"Then we talked to Mr. Bill Storm," Corey said, "but he didn't have any idea why someone would have the number back then. He did say his father, Mr. Fred Storm, might know something. Mr. Storm took us to meet his father, and when we told Mr. Fred what we'd found out, he started crying and saying it shouldn't have happened."

"That's when he told us how Phillip Cooper got up into the clock tower," he continued.

Corey told the whole story, using his notes when he couldn't remember something. He tried to make sure everyone understood how Phillip was trapped because the old latch accidently locked, just like it did on him and Michelle.

Michelle told the part about Mr. Fred being slapped and locked in his room for two days, so he never got the chance to tell anyone.

"Mr. Fred told us he was scared," she said, "but also said with everything else happening, he didn't think anyone would listen."

"I bet they would have," Judge Danielson said. "After all, you've got proof Arthur Cooper did report his son missing."

"Yeah, but Mr. Cooper was killed a few days later," Corey said, "and nothing happened after that."

"So what happened?" Michelle asked, "Why didn't people keep looking?

"Why didn't anyone keep asking about Phillip Cooper disappearing?"

"Maybe they *did* think he'd just run away after his father was killed," Marybelle said.

Judge Barker chuckled, "I think it's a little more than that," he said.

No one spoke for several seconds. Judge Barker looked at the others for some recognition, but found none.

"I think it's right here in front of us," he said, "and I'm surprised the rest of you don't see it."

"I don't know what you mean," Judge Danielson said. The others looked at Barker.

"It's the dates," Barker said. "When Phillip Cooper disappeared and when that was reported in the paper."

Everyone, including Corey and Michelle looked at the copied articles.

"He disappeared on Wednesday, the twentieth," Corey said.

"And it was reported in the paper on Friday," Michelle added, "November 22, 1963."

Geltsin's eyebrows went up. Judge Danielson nodded his head and smiled. Mrs. Palmer and Mrs. Pritchard didn't react.

"That's right," Barker said, "and what else happened that day?"

Corey and Michelle looked at each other.

"Don't they teach you American history in school?" Barker said.

"Yes, sir," Corey said, "but we haven't gotten that far. It's been mostly about the Revolutionary War and on up. We haven't done much from the last century."

"What happened that day?" Michelle asked. "Why is the date important?"

"Young lady," Judge Barker said, "that is one of the most important and remembered dates in the last one hundred years.

"That's the day the President of the United States was shot and killed."

Both kids grew wide-eyed.

Judge Barker rose and went to the bookshelves along the wall. He pulled down the volume for *K* from the set of encyclopedias there and opened it to the entry on President Kennedy. He set the open book in front of Corey and Michelle.

"I'm not your teacher," he told them, "so I won't make you look it up yourself. But here's the basic story."

"And I'm really surprised you don't know about it already." The judge sat down again.

"Now I'm likely the only one here old enough to remember that day," Barker continued. "But I do remember it well. Sort of like the way we all remember nine-eleven."

Annette and Marybelle looked at each other nodding. They certainly did. They were both pregnant at the time and stuck at home with little else to do but watch television.

"Of course, it didn't happen around here," Barker said. "Our day was going along like most Fridays, but when the news came, everything stopped. The whole country ground to a halt for several days. Everyone either watched TV or talked about what happened."

"It didn't even matter what people thought about President Kennedy," the judge continued. "He was the President, and people didn't know what would happen to the country.

"Things didn't start getting back to normal until after the big funeral the next week. And by then, it seems, Phillip's father was dead, and the Thanksgiving holiday rolled around, and so it's possible our missing youngster just got lost in the shuffle of everything."

"But it's not fair," Michelle said. "It's not right. No one should be forgotten about like that and lost for so long.

"Someone should have kept looking for him."

Corey nodded in agreement.

"My dear," Judge Barker said, "I think you are right. I also think that's the real lesson in all this. No one should ever be forgotten."

"And because of you two," Judge Danielson said, "he hasn't been. He's been found.

"You've brought a young man home." No one spoke for several seconds.

"You've done a wonderful job with all of this," Danielson continued, "wouldn't everyone agree?"

The others nodded.

"What will happen to Mr. Fred?" Michelle asked.

The judges looked at each other.

"Probably nothing," Danielson said. "The medical examiner's report says young Cooper died from injuries to his head and his hand. Not because Fred Storm never told anyone. It was an accident, kids; I don't think Mr. Storm will face any charges."

"And it was a long time ago," Judge Barker added. "He was still a child where the law is concerned. I'm pretty sure the County Prosecutor will see it that way."

"But there's a good story here," Geltsin said, gathering his notes. He noticed the silence and looked up. Everyone was staring at him.

"What's the matter?" he asked.

"I think our two young friends are concerned about the last part of the story coming out," Judge Danielson said.

"Oh, don't worry," Geltsin said. "Bill Storm is my friend too. I won't do anything with that until I talk to him first."

He looked at Corey and Michelle "Now I'm still going to need some help from you two."

"What can we do?" Corey said.

"First off, I need a list of everyone you talked to so I can follow up. Then, I'll need to talk to you again for some more details."

"And you, young lady," he said, pointing at Michelle. "Please remember what you said a minute ago. I think you're right. It's a lesson we all need to learn."

"Do I have copies of everything you came up with?" he asked, organizing his papers and notebook.

"Yes, sir," Corey said, "You already have the forensic file."

"Thanks, kids," he said, "I'll talk to you later."

After the editor left, Corey and Michelle quietly began putting all their things back in the boxes. Annette and Marybelle began cleaning up the lunch debris and leftovers.

"Why so glum, you two?" Judge Danielson asked. "Like I said, you did a great job. You've found someone lost for over fifty years and solved a mystery."

"And please don't worry about old Fred Storm," he added. "He'll be fine."

"We know," Corey said.

"So what's wrong?"

"We don't have anything else to do," Michelle said, "and we're still grounded for the rest of the summer."

"Is that so?" Judge Barker said. "That's interesting."

"Judge Danielson," he continued, "I don't know about you, but if someone came before my court having shown the dedication and hard work these two have, I'd be inclined to commute their sentences to time served or discharge their parole. What do you think?"

"Well now, Your Honor," Judge Danielson said, "I don't think it's our place to tell parents how to discipline their children, but I have to say that given the way you've presented the matter, I'd be inclined to agree with you.

"Of course we probably do need to send this matter to the proper authorities, don't you think, ladies?"

Annette and Marybelle stopped wrapping the leftover salad.

"Are you saying we should unground them? Annette asked.

"I think you might consider it," Danielson said. "They've shown remarkable initiative, they've behaved well, for the most part, and I think they've learned some important lessons over these past weeks."

"Mom?" Corey said.

Annette looked at Marybelle. She nodded.

"Alright, your grounding's rescinded. You're back to regular rules."

The whoop Corey let out would have brought proceedings to a halt in other courtrooms, but fortunately, they were emptied for the lunch break.

Michelle ran over and hugged her mother.

"Can we go home and change now?" she asked.

"No," Annette said, "you first need to get all this stuff down to the office."

"No problem," Corey said, quickly putting things away.

"And you're still restricted on your phone and laptop, Michelle," Marybelle said.

"You too, Corey," Annette added.

"Race you home," Corey said to Michelle.

"No fair!" Michelle said. "You're taller and you run faster."

"I'll take you home," Marybelle said. "It's safer that way."

"Why don't you take these boxes too?" Annette said.

"Leave an extra copy of everything for me," Judge Danielson said. "I'll send it over to the chief to put in his files."

They couldn't run down the main stairs with the boxes, but Corey and Michelle went down to the first floor as fast as they could. Mrs. Pritchard was out of breath when she caught up.

After walking down to the library and stowing things in the trunk, Marybelle drove the kids home. She dropped Corey off first.

"I'll change, grab my bike, and meet you at your house," he said.

"Great," Michelle said, "what do you want to do?"

"Let's ride up to Lake Cyrus and see what's going on."

"Okay, see you in a few."

XVI

Richard Geltsin talked to Bill Storm the next day. After hearing what the judges said, the druggist agreed to let the paper include Fred's story. Geltsin wouldn't say anything about Bill's grandfather's actions.

He then spent several weeks following up with the people the kids spoke to. He interviewed the ladies in the records office, Chief Blaise, Sheriff Wingate, Officer Shelton, and Doctor Driscoll.

Officer Shelton combined the files Judge Danielson sent over with her very slim report and placed the now closed case information into storage. She entered all the information into her computer, too.

Geltsin e-mailed back and forth with Corey and Michelle getting more details on their adventure in the tower and talked to Mr. Hingstrom for more about the clock itself.

The editor interviewed Ethel Cooper, too, even though it cost him an expensive lunch at the Majestic Hotel. Corey and Michelle were invited as well, and that meant another summer day wearing their Sunday best.

To Corey's dismay, Josie Cooper wasn't available to bring Miss Ethel in the old Polara. Lela drove her down the hill in the Camry and joined the lunch.

To expand the story, Geltsin also interviewed older residents in the area for their recollections of John F. Kennedy's assassination. While some people didn't have the fondest memories of the thirty-fifth President, most confirmed what Judge Barker said earlier. Everything came to a complete stop for several days that November. No one thought of anything else until the holiday.

Geltsin carefully wrote Fred Storm's part in the affair, trying not to mention how the two boys were both involved. He left it that Fred and Phil were friends and Fred did know Phil wanted to explore the

tower.

> *According to his son, Fred Storm knew his friend wanted to explore the clock tower, but never knew if Phillip Cooper ever attempted it.*
>
> *William Storm, 41 and the current proprietor of Storm's Drugs in Craigsville, stated he'd heard the story several times over the years, but neither he nor his father knew what became of Cooper until the body was recently discovered.*
>
> *"Dad always guessed Phil ran away after his father died," the younger Mr. Storm said.*
>
> *Fred Storm, 65, currently resides at Magnolia Valley Nursing Home where he has lived since suffering major injuries in an explosion and fire eleven years ago.*
>
> *He was not well enough to be interviewed for this story.*

The story ran on Labor Day under the editor's by-line, though

Geltsin listed the kids as co-authors. The paper printed it as a

special pull-out section. Maybe people would want to keep it.

The editor also hoped other newspapers in the region would

want it as well and several did, so the *Record / Times* enjoyed a

small spike in circulation. Other papers, including the big one from

the state capitol, asked for electronic versions to post on their

websites, as did one national cable news outlet.

Though many Coopers still lived in the area, no one remained

from that branch of the family to do conclusive DNA testing. The closest relations were third and fourth cousins, a couple of generations removed. Still, though, everyone accepted the body the kids found was indeed Phillip E. Cooper. Later in September, Miss Ethel arranged for the remains to be buried in the family plot at Eden Valley. The young man was laid to rest next to Arthur Cooper.

The story made Corey and Michelle minor celebrities as school. Even their social studies teacher told them it was good work, and changed the class schedule to talk about the event in November. Unfortunately, all the notoriety meant they couldn't use the adventure as a class project. They ended up needing to find something else for their research project in the spring.

Fred Storm passed away peacefully in January of the next year. His doctor said his lungs just couldn't keep up anymore and the stress simply wore his heart out. Fred never mentioned Phillip Cooper or the incident again, but when the people at Magnolia Valley went through his belongings, they found a copy of the story carefully folded and tucked into a hardback book.

The old clock kept running smoothly and everyone still checked their watch when the bell tolled on the hour and half-hour. By

Thanksgiving, though, folks began commenting on how the chimes seemed to be a bit more accurate.